HOME IS
THE HEART

HOME IS THE HEART

•

Ellen Gray Massey

AVALON BOOKS
THOMAS BOUREGY AND COMPANY, INC.
401 LAFAYETTE STREET
NEW YORK, NEW YORK 10003

PRINTED IN THE UNITED STATES OF AMERICA
ON ACID-FREE PAPER
BY HADDON CRAFTSMEN, BLOOMSBURG, PENNSYLVANIA

To my sister-in-law, Ethel Massey,
my model for Darrah's great-aunt.

Chapter One

"Darrah, I can't tell you how much it means to me that you're bringing me back here," my great-aunt Iris said as we drove down the highway into her old neighborhood.

She was like an eager child anticipating Santa Claus. She didn't miss a single house or driveway turning off into the woods, telling me who lived there years ago. As we got closer to the lane turning off to her old home, she sobered when she realized how things had changed. The Carlton house was run-down and deserted, its once well-kept yard a wilderness of brush, cedars, and vines. Elbow Jurgen's house was completely done over with aluminum siding and room additions, so that Iris hardly recognized it. The road leading to the old Stony Ridge School had a fence across it. It was obvious there had been no traffic that way in years. Just before we crossed Dibben's Creek and the bottom fields leading to the river, we noticed

1

that a cousin and his wife had built three huge silos down the hill from their house.

But the river was the same. Iris breathed in satisfaction when she looked first up the stream and then down. I stopped on the low-water bridge so she could enjoy the view longer.

"Arnie and I used to fish right there in that hole of water," she said, pointing downstream to a secluded spot visible from just the one point on the bridge where we paused. She laughed, probably at the memory of a childhood secret with her long-dead brother. "This is more like it should be," she said.

Then she gasped in pleasure as a large blue heron landed on the gravel bar and waded into the same fishing spot. Unperturbed by my car stopped on the concrete bridge just a few inches above the water, the bird ducked his head and pulled out a flopping perch.

The heron and the pull up the hill out of the river bottom restored her happy mood. At the crest of the hill, we turned off the blacktop and rattled over the cattle guard into a country lane. This was her home ground—no tumbledown or remodeled buildings there to change the landscape that was etched in her memory. The exposed bluff and the rounded, wooded hills were just as she remembered.

So was most of the two-mile drive down the one-lane road toward her old farm home. I reminded her that Gee Chester's house was gone. Also his log barn that we always used to drive around just before we slowed to descend the hill to reach the old place. She was prepared for that, for she knew they had been gone for many years, even though she hadn't been back. We rolled down our windows to enjoy the fresh autumn temperature.

As I drove slowly over the rough lane, careful to avoid the chug holes, she sat on the edge of the seat, her white head turning from side to side to take in everything. The branches of the tall oak trees above us touched my car. Goldenrod, white asters, and blue chicory crowded the lane in spots that the sun reached. A red fox squirrel jumped from one tree to another crossing the road ahead of us. A brown rabbit scurried into the brush, scaring up a covey of quail. We heard the flutter of their wings as they took flight and disappeared in the trees.

"I know every inch of this road, Darrah girl," Iris said, smiling. "I've walked it many and many a day coming after the mail."

Her excitement infected me. I had some childhood memories of traveling the lane too, but my main enjoyment was seeing the profusion of plants all about us. I noticed the orange-yellow blossoms of oxeye, clusters of gray coneflowers, and some red butterfly weed still in bloom. My delight was complete when I spotted a hazelnut bush. Perhaps on the way back I could stop to collect some seed to add these native plants to my nursery inventory.

Aunt Iris leaned forward until her forehead was almost against the windshield. "Go slow up here just after we turn into our old driveway and start down the hill. This is the best part."

I remembered the spot she was referring to. Her home buildings were built on the benchland just far enough above the river-bottom fields to be out of reach of the highest flood. Though we'd already crossed the river on the blacktop, we couldn't follow it to the farm. The highway climbed out of the valley to the ridge. Then from the cattle guard on top of the hill, the lane we were on followed the crest of the ridge. Private drives led off that lane to the farms along the river, the only good farming land in this rugged Ozark landscape.

Just after we left the ridge lane and turned into the narrower driveway to her old place, there was an open meadow where we would have a panoramic view of the whole Loveland farm—the two-story, white frame house, large oak barn and concrete silo, several outbuildings, and, of course, beyond them, the checkered fields of corn, soybeans, and hay. All this scene was framed on the east by the darker green line of trees obscuring the river.

"Do you suppose the people who own our place now will let us go into the house?" Iris asked. She had lived there all her life until her late sixties, when both her parents died.

"Probably." I was almost as eager to see the view again as she. I had many childhood memories of my visits: listening to my great-grandfather's exciting stories, eating wonderful dinners there, playing with lots of cousins, exploring the caves, and swimming in the river. I hadn't been there myself since Aunt Iris left twenty years ago. "But Aunt Iris," I said, thinking of the Jurgen and Carlton places we'd just passed, "they may have changed it. It might not look like it used to."

She looked at me and shook her head slightly with

an of-course-I-know-that expression. Then she put her hand on the leg of my black jeans and patted it slightly to show her pleasure in being here and to thank me for bringing her. For years at family gatherings she had said that just once more before she died she wanted to see the old place. No one paid any attention to her—me included. But at the last family gathering I was surprised to see how frail she was. Always dependent on someone in the family to drive her, she asked me to take her. Having no good reason not to, I left with a vague promise to come take her when the weather cooled.

This morning she'd called to ask if I was busy and would I drive her there. Yes, I was busy, but I couldn't refuse her. I don't remember her ever asking me to do anything for her before. She was getting so crippled that I was afraid that in a few more months she wouldn't be able to go. So since my partner and I run our own landscaping business, I postponed mulching the plantings at the Griffins' new house to pick her up at Grove Ridge. We shortened the name of her little town to The Grove.

Just as we started down the old driveway, after cresting the hill that overlooked the old homestead, I was too occupied in missing a box turtle and looking into my rearview mirror to see that I didn't run over him to notice Aunt Iris's reaction. I didn't see her face when the farm came into view, but I felt her hand tightening on my leg, almost pinching it. She gasped and tried ineffectively to raise herself from the seat. I braked to a standstill and looked at her. Her eyes were staring ahead and her mouth was open as if the words she was planning to say froze. She was trembling.

Startled at her reaction, I looked out over the drop in the edge of the drive and over the fifteen acres of meadow slanting down to the farm. I expected to see the old house, the maple trees surrounding it, the huge ponderosa pine by the front gate, some flowers, side-walks, and the lawn fence, with the barn and other outbuildings farther back. I even wondered if the old iron hand pump that fascinated me as a child would still be on the well curb by the front yard gate.

Nothing! I blinked my eyes, shook my head, and to see more clearly, I pushed back the lock of red hair that always fell over my forehead. I was right the first time. Nothing. No house, no fence, no barn or other buildings, no trees. Not a stump or any evidence of concrete foundations. Nowhere in the entire landscape was there an accumulation of boards or roofing or even tree limbs. Not a trace that this had once been a busy farmstead. The seven-acre area where the build-ings once stood was a huge, deep pond not quite full of water. The scattered clouds lazing across the sky were reflected on its surface. The red, subsoil dirt and clay banks contained not a blade of grass or a bush to soften their rawness.

"Gone," Aunt Iris moaned. "It's all gone."

She slumped against the seat, laying her head back against the headrest. She squeezed her eyes closed tight like a little girl. The wrinkles on her forehead and cheeks deepened as she closed up her face in her determination not to see. She put her hands over her eyes. "Turn around. I can't look anymore." She began to sob softly. "I shouldn't have come."

"I'm sorry, Aunt Iris," I said, wanting to put my arms around her. We were both in shock. Surely at least one of us in the family would have heard something. None of us lived very far away, and we still knew a few of the old neighbors. Did the house and barn burn down? Were they torn down?

The earth seemed to fall out from under me. I never lived there. I only visited, but precious to me were my early childhood memories of going to Gramps's and Granny's, my great-grandparents, when Aunt Iris did most of their work on the farm. Up till now, just knowing the place still existed gave me roots. The solidarity of the farm buildings proved my heritage. I could only imagine Aunt Iris's feelings—she had lived there most of her life. Because she often shared her memories about the farm, I knew she thought about it a great deal during the years after she moved into a little house in The Grove. Her house was comfortable, but it wasn't home. The farm was home. Now it didn't exist.

"Please, Darrah girl, turn around." Aunt Iris still didn't open her eyes. She kept both hands clamped over her face like she used to do when playing hide-and-seek with me and my cousins just before she would call out, "Here I come, ready or not!" Then she used to open her eyes and pretend not to see us lurking behind trees while she looked in all the wrong places. This time when she opened her eyes she didn't have to pretend. She wouldn't see what she was looking for.

Even with my little car, I couldn't turn around where I had stopped in the narrow driveway. If I continued forward, the only place to turn around was at the gate to the farm. A quick glance told me that even the gate wasn't there anymore. Rather than prolong Aunt Iris's agony, I put my car in reverse. The wheels spun on the rocky surface until they dug in enough to get traction to back up the hill. As rapidly as I could, craning my neck to see behind and glancing at my rearview mirror, I backed up to a slightly wider place in the drive where I had about two feet in which to maneuver to get turned around. Carefully I started to ease back and forth several times.

Neither of us said anything more. As I was manipulating the car, I sensed her mood. As she had had to do many times in her life, she held herself rigid. Accepting the razed homestead was just another trial she would have to get through. In her late eighties, coping was getting harder and harder to do.

We were both still so stunned from the emptiness where once there had been so much, that we didn't see or hear anything else. My tires were spewing out gravel as I seesawed across the drive to turn around. What attention I had was watching to see that I didn't drop off the drive into the meadow, which was now behind us, or get stuck in the gravel and dirt the grader had piled on the high side of the drive.

Now facing the woods instead of the farm scene, Aunt Iris dropped her hands from her face. She smoothed back her rumpled, short hair. It was white and straight, but it used to be red like mine.

"Darrah girl!" Aunt Iris suddenly screamed. She

grabbed my knee. ''O-o-oh!'' On my right, I heard a screech of brakes and the grating of tires shrieking to a stop. An angry truck horn blared unceasingly. The discord seemed to come from my own car. Not understanding, I stared at my steering wheel to see if I was pressing the horn. Then I saw, just inches from Aunt Iris's door, and completely blocking the view from her window, the grille of a black Ford pickup. In the dust kicked up by the truck's abrupt stop, a man jumped out of the driver's side, slammed his door angrily, and sprinted around both vehicles to my window.

''What are you doing blocking the drive like that?'' he shouted through my open window. ''I could have killed you both!'' His face was flushed as he jerked off his cap and ran his fingers through his brown hair in frustration. He shot a quick glance down the steep meadow hill where, without his quick reflexes and excellent brakes, both of our vehicles would have been turning over and over toward the hateful pond.

''I was just turning around.'' Even as I said it I knew how ridiculous that sounded. No sensible person would turn around on a blind hill in a drive that was scarcely wider than the length of the car, especially when there was a wide-open space down the drive about two hundred yards at the foot of the hill.

''Turning around right here!'' The tall, slim man spread out both his hands in exasperation. He wasn't quite so upset with us now that he saw that we were two women, and one of us elderly. ''And what the blazes are you doing way out here, anyway? Are you lost?'' He looked past me to peer more closely at my great-aunt, who was still slumped in her seat to protect herself from the inevitable collision. She appeared even smaller than she was.

"No, young man," Aunt Iris said, pulling herself erect and thrusting back her head. Her hazel eyes glared straight at him even though she couldn't help seeing behind him the nothingness that was once her home. "No, we aren't lost." She spoke slowly, emphasizing each word. "I was born here. Right down there, and for years I lived in the house that is gone. When I saw that atrocious, ugly pond, I couldn't bear to go a single foot farther, so we turned around." She glared at him, daring him to object to her logic. When he dropped his hands to his side and nodded his head just slightly in acknowledgment, she added in a less determined tone, "Now, if you will please move your pickup, we'll leave."

The man took a few steps back. His brown eyes studied both of us for a couple of seconds. Without saying another word, he touched the brim of his cap and walked back to his truck. He backed up the drive much more skillfully and quickly than I had done until he found a place wide enough for us to pass. He pulled over as close to the trees as he could get.

I had to back up two more times to get headed up the hill. I crept past his truck. I had only about three inches between our two vehicles and the same space between my right tires and the edge of the drive that dropped off into the steep meadow. When I pulled up even with his window I slowed almost to a stop.

I wasn't sure whether I was in the wrong or the man was. I'd learned when in a confrontation to either thank the other person or apologize. One or the other response usually defused any anger. In this case I did both. Through my still-opened window I said, "Thank you." When he nodded slightly in response, I added, "I'm sorry."

"No harm done," he said. His face no longer showed anger or exasperation. Perhaps his earlier expression had been worry. His eyebrows were still lowered and his eyes partially squinted. At my words, his brows relaxed and his lips turned up just slightly at each corner. Not a true smile, but one that relaxed his face.

As I drove away, I kept him in view in my side mirror. He was apparently watching us, for he didn't start up his truck. At the top of the hill, I turned on the ridge lane into the woods where I could no longer see him or the ruined view of the valley. I drove back to the blacktop as quickly as I could, completely out of the mood of stopping to collect seeds from the flowers along the lane.

"You all right?" I asked Aunt Iris.

"Yes, I'm fine."

I glanced over at her. She did seem okay. The horror was gone from her face, though her hands were tightly clasped in her lap. She was gazing at the woods again, not with the anticipation she had when we came, but with an air of resignation.

"I shouldn't have brought you here without checking it out first. My fault. I never dreamed . . ."

"It's all right, Darrah girl. Really. That young man was right. There's no harm done." She held on to the assist handle as I swerved to miss a chug hole. "It isn't all gone just now, child. It's been gone a long time.''

She didn't have to explain. I knew she meant her old life on the farm.

She nodded her head slightly. ''Yes. I've known that in my mind, of course, but somehow I never really accepted it. When you have one life for more than sixty-five years, you can't easily let it go just like that.''

I understood. Aunt Iris never went to high school, never traveled farther than fifty miles from home, never had an outside job off the farm other than helping out occasionally with a sick neighbor, and she never married. She was the mainstay for her parents, in the home and on the farm. She cared for her younger siblings. When they grew up and left home, she cared for her aging parents. When they died, she couldn't handle the farm alone. With her share of its sale, she bought a little house in The Grove. In the twenty years since then, she had never been back.

I was trying to decide whether the trip was a tragedy. Aunt Iris had lost too many crops from drought or flood to brood over losses. In addition to her parents, she lost two baby brothers and two grown brothers, one of them my own grandfather who died before I was born, plus many other relatives and neighbors. She saw their first barn burn from a lightning strike. Therefore, finding an ugly, raw earth embankment of a new pond where she expected to see her birthplace was just another hurdle she would overcome.

''Did you notice that the fields looked good?'' she asked. Her voice was normal.

"No, I was too shocked to see the buildings gone to look."

"Whoever owns the place is caring for the land. The pasture has more grass than I've ever seen and all the brush is cleared out."

I knew then that I had done the right thing in bringing her. She wasn't someone to be shielded.

"Did you know that young man?" Aunt Iris asked. Her mood changed quickly to a lighter tone.

Surprised at the change of subject, I said, "No, why?"

"Just wondered. Fine-looking fellow, don't you think? Probably on his way to the river to go fishing. I noticed he had a minnow bucket and some other fishing gear in his truck."

I looked at her in amazement. "I thought you had your eyes shut tight so you wouldn't see."

She ignored me. Her normal spirit was back. "And he's got money. His jeans and shirt were designer clothes."

"How do you know that?"

"Not much to do anymore. I read and watch a lot of television. He didn't buy those clothes from Wal-Mart."

We crossed the cattle guard and turned onto the blacktop. I drove rapidly back to The Grove. "Okay, Miss Detective, what else did you notice about him?"

"I noticed, Darrah girl, that he wasn't wearing a wedding ring."

Chapter Two

I couldn't stop thinking about the Loveland farm and its lost buildings. I called around to my relatives. None of them knew about it, and since it had changed hands a few times since we sold it, we'd lost track of who owned it. And like my Aunt Iris, none of us had been back. A couple of cousins still fished down on the river, but they put their canoes in the water at the low-water bridge and floated downstream. From the river the buildings were not visible.

The next day on the way to the Griffins' house to finish up the job I had postponed to take Aunt Iris to the farm, I called my great-aunt on my cell phone to see how she was feeling after her excursion and bombshell surprise.

"I don't fret about it," she told me. "We sold the farm, so it's not for us to say anymore."

"But I can't stand thinking about what those buildings represented. All that history, the activity, the good

14

times, all the living, the birthing, and even the dying, that went on there for six generations. Then with a few swaths of a bulldozer, it's all gone.''

''Just the buildings, Darrah girl, just the buildings. The land is still there. And our family. It's still here.''

''But . . .''

''You were old enough to understand. Don't you remember? We decided it was best to sell after my father died. None of us could keep it up. It's better to have the buildings gone than rotting down like we saw yesterday on the old Carlton place with the land all growing up in brush. It's even better than having the buildings modernized so that we don't recognize them, like Elbow Jurgen's. The land is what is important. The land on our old place is being cared for. I saw that.''

''Maybe someday I can . . .'' I didn't finish, for I really didn't know what I meant. Did I really want to own the farm myself? I used to ask my father why he didn't buy it. His answers were vague: that he couldn't afford it, and he was too busy with his job to take care of it.

I also used to dream that if I owned it, and had enough money, that I could turn it into a museum to show how people used to farm with horses and hand labor. But that dream wasn't possible anymore. The buildings with all the old farming tools and equipment were gone.

Aunt Iris was telling me how good it was that the land was cared for. And so it was. We both noticed that in spite of our astonishment. Maybe . . . A different dream was forming in my head. Maybe if I owned it, I could turn it into a sort of natural preserve. The farm possessed all the interesting characteristics of Ozark karst topography—a river, springs, caves, sinkholes, bluffs, glades, and forests. As a landscape designer specializing in native plants, I knew that possibility was well within my expertise. I began to get excited as ideas and potentials popped into my head. I could identify all the native plants, reintroduce others that had disappeared over the years, return the whole 160 acres to its native state, and open it for—

"Forget about it," Aunt Iris said, as if she was reading my mind over the telephone. "There's nothing you can do about it. Besides, you've got a good business yourself and your whole life ahead of you. Spend your energies working on your future. The past is gone. You can't hold on to it, and it shouldn't protrude to ruin your present." She paused before hanging up. "Thanks for taking me back once more. That was all I wanted. I won't ask again."

Of course she is right, I told myself. When I get with some of my family, I get hung up on all that nostalgia stuff. But it is such a cool farm and has so many memories for all of us. Aunt Iris gives good advice. I've got more important things to attend to. My partner, Connie, and I are paying off our loans for our landscaping business, which is now doing well enough for us to have two crews of full-time help, plus a woman working full-time to take care of greenhouses. We've both been totally busy all this season except for a short slump during a couple of hot July weeks. And now, the coolness and the good rains we've enjoyed after a dry summer have put planting back in people's minds. We are grateful that we already have a few small jobs lined up to do before freezing weather.

I felt a little better after Iris's reassurance and my reasoning. Pleased with Connie's and my success and proud of our new, extended-bed pickup with our business name printed on both doors, I shook my head to rid it of these fantasies about the Loveland farm. I reviewed my schedule for the day.

Just before I turned into the Griffins' drive to finish the mulching job, I received a call. "We're magic. This is Darrah from Magic Landscaping. How may I help you?"

"I understand that you specialize in using native flora in your planting designs," a man's voice said.

"Well, yes, we do use native plants when we can. They are hardy and have a greater survival rate." I was immediately impressed that he used the term "flora." "We have many species in our nursery. Are you wanting to plant some dogwood or redbud?" Those two trees were the usual ones most people wanted.

"Oh, much more than that. I already have quite a few of them. What I've got is a hundred acres including woodlands, rocky glades, and some open pasture. I want to restore it to the way it was when the Osages and Bluff Dwellers lived here. Return the pasture to prairie grasses and replant in the woods some of the native trees and forbs that have disappeared."

I was really impressed that he knew about the pre-European people who lived here. I was doubly impressed at his differentiation between grasses and other small plants.

"That sounds like a great plan."

"Yes. And I want to do some extensive plantings and landscaping in the entrance to my place. This is a seven- or eight-acre area that is virtually bare now."

"I see." I was elated. What a coincidence! What he wanted sounded like what I was just daydreaming about wanting to do myself on the Loveland family farm. Here was an opportunity to try out my ideas, and for pay! This was a job that would keep us busy all winter. The figures were scrolling up in my mind as I estimated the thousands of dollars' worth of plants and labor involved.

"Your firm has come well recommended," the voice continued. "Are you equipped to handle a job on that big a scale?" He didn't pause to hear my answer and couldn't see me nodding my head off. "I don't want to do it all at once, but I'd want a total plan drawn up with an estimate as quickly as possible. Then, if feasible, start out with some aspects of it this fall and winter."

"And how! All right!" I barely breathed the words into the phone in my enthusiasm. I almost dropped my cell phone while all at the same time juggling it, my elation, and the turn into the Griffins' drive. Then assuming my professional voice and speaking louder so he could hear, I assured him, "We can handle that, I'm sure." His laughter told me that he'd heard my first gleeful exclamation. I pretended that I didn't notice his amusement and pressed on in my businesslike manner, though I couldn't keep the excitement out of my voice as I spoke rapidly. "Right now in early fall is an excellent time of the year to start. Doing it in phases is also a very good way to do the job. I always draw up a master plan with estimates first, so that is no problem. My partner and I could meet with you on . . ." I stopped my pickup and fumbled on the passenger's seat for my appointment book.

"Wednesday morning at nine o'clock?" the man asked. "I can meet with you then."

That time was already scheduled, but what the heck? For a job of this magnitude we could reschedule. "Sure," I said. "That will be fine."

"I was told how knowledgeable you are about plants and that your work is unusual and imaginative."

I laughed self-consciously, but was proud that we'd earned that sort of reputation. "We try."

"And that you are enthusiastic." He chuckled. "I can tell that you are."

"Oh, yes." I could hardly wait for this conversation to be over so I could call Connie. But I knew I shouldn't sound too eager and childlike. That distinguished-sounding man might think we were too inexperienced to undertake such a big job. I pegged him as in his sixties, probably with wavy, silver hair. I toned down my voice. "We enjoy our work. We make things more beautiful while helping the ecology. What you want sounds wonderful."

"Good. I'll show you just what I have in mind. Then when you get your estimate done, we'll see. I assume that you charge a fee for the estimate?"

We never had. Connie kept telling me we should.

"Yes, a hundred dollars down payment." No time like
the present to start a new policy.

He didn't flinch. "That's agreeable." He said his
name was Moss Wright. He suggested we meet at a
country store south of town on the state highway so
we could follow him to his property. "It's difficult to
give directions to my place. It would be better that we
meet and you follow me." He started to tell me where
the store was, until I told him I was quite familiar with
it. "Good. Wednesday at nine it is." He hung up.

Moss Wright. I couldn't remember anyone with that
name. There were some Wrights in the county, a high
school teacher, and an older couple I'd done some
pruning work for, but I couldn't recall anyone named
Moss. Probably one of the newcomers. He definitely
didn't have the local accent. Many of our big clients
were these new people who expected to spend money
to make their lawns beautiful. The local people were
less willing to hire someone to do landscape work.
Probably a holdover from the self-sufficient farm life-
style when the family did all the work themselves.
They didn't have time to take care of nonessentials
like ornamental planting.

However, that attitude was changing. I hoped that
Magic Landscaping had a hand in that. Our beautiful
landscaping on the newcomers' lawns was beginning
to change the local people's attitudes, inspiring them
to improve their own lawns. Perhaps my great-
grandfather had helped inspire *his* neighbors. He was
different from most men. Gramps planted perennials
and annuals all along the fencerow. I pictured the lawn
of the old home place as I remembered it. He

had lilac and barberry bushes banking the front porch and hard maple trees shading a bluegrass lawn. Crowning all was a tall pine tree.

I was so excited about our new job prospect that I ran to the area where I had to do some finishing touches on the mulching job. What a coup, having an entire hundred acres to work on! Maybe I could write it up in one of the major landscaping magazines! I couldn't wait to tell Connie.

Connie and I had met in design classes at the university and were both active in the scuba diving club. When I told her about the twenty acres I inherited from my parents near Timberton, my hometown, and my idea of starting a landscaping business there, she was interested. We became full partners. We started with my land and her capital, plus borrowing more. We remodeled my little barn into an office and potting room, erected three plastic-covered greenhouses, bought a secondhand truck and tractor, and invested in nursery stock. I lived in the four-room house on the place. She rented an apartment nearby.

We had a tough couple of years at first. Though we were the only landscaping firm within fifty miles, the people weren't accustomed to spending money on their lawns except for mowing and raking leaves— which we didn't do. We subsisted on pruning and replacement work. We also had to overcome the prejudice that women shouldn't dig, operate the dump truck, tractor, and other big equipment, or do all the heavy, outdoor work involved with landscaping. Though Connie was tall, our credibility was further hampered by my being only five feet, one inch tall.

Our having workers to do much of the heavy work didn't seem to matter. The occasional big job from a newcomer kept us afloat the first two years.

Connie was even more excited than I was about our new client. She was worried about our year-end finances and how we could save enough money to restock our nursery for next spring's rush. This account with Mr. Wright would put us in the black enough to pay off some more of our debts.

On Wednesday we drove our pickup the ten miles south of town to the meeting place. Since we were early, we went inside to get a cold drink and visit with the storekeeper, a distant relative of mine. We hadn't been there five minutes before we heard a vehicle come to an abrupt stop in front.

"That must be our client," Connie said, and hurried outside to greet him. His being early seemed a good omen to both of us.

I finished my conversation with the storekeeper and followed her, expecting to see the distinguished older man I had envisioned and his well-dressed wife. But facing the door of the store as he talked with Connie was the fisherman who almost ran into Aunt Iris and me at the Loveland farm. We both stopped in astonishment. He looked at me with a half-surprised and half-curious expression.

"Darrah, this is Moss Wright," Connie said. "He told me that he's recently bought the . . ." She paused when she noticed that we were staring at each other, he with the half frown he wore with Aunt Iris, and I gaping at him with my mouth open. So this was the guy that . . .

"Did you catch any fish?" I asked, forcing my voice to be pleasant. It was a stupid thing to say, but it was the first thing that came into my mind.

"What?" Mr. Wright asked.

"My aunt thought you were going fishing down on the river. She saw fishing gear in your pickup."

"Oh that! No, I didn't fish any that day."

"Darrah!" Not knowing about our recent run-in, Connie punched me before I'd say something else stupid and completely ruin this job prospect. "He recently bought the old Loveland place on the river." Then the idea suddenly dawned on her. "Does that have any connection to your family?"

Mr. Wright was watching me closely, obviously putting together our confrontation in the farm driveway and what Aunt Iris had said to him about being born there. "If I'm not mistaken," he said to Connie while still studying me, "my place used to belong to someone in her family, right?"

Connie clapped her hand over her mouth as if that action might prevent what would come out of mine.

I nodded. "I am Darrah Loveland."

"A grandfather?" he asked.

"Close. It belonged to my great-grandfather." I controlled my emotions even though it was obvious that this was the man who had violated the home place. Wondering how I could work with someone who had leveled our family homestead, I made myself assume my business mode. "I'm happy to formally meet you, Mr. Wright. Shall we go to the farm now?" I couldn't force myself to say, "go to *your* place."

I held out my hand. He took it in his firm grip. Then

addressing both of us, he said, "I'll go first, though obviously you know the way."

We retraced the route Aunt Iris and I had traveled just two days before. When we turned off the blacktop at the cattle guard onto the narrow, graveled lane, I slowed to avoid the dust kicked up by his pickup.

"What's this all about?" Connie asked. Though she had lived in the county for a few years, she long ago gave up trying to keep straight all my many relatives. She vowed that I was kin to half the people in the county. She was almost right. Loveland is a common name. I was probably related in some way to all of them down to fifth or sixth cousins. When Mr. Wright had told her that he bought the old Loveland farm, she didn't connect it with my family. There were a dozen farms owned by Lovelands. We even did some work on a couple of them.

Nor had I had an opportunity to tell her about Aunt Iris's and my visit to our old family farm. I probably wouldn't have anyway, for whenever I started to say anything about my family, she would adopt her martyred look and throw up her hands. Having no family herself, she couldn't understand how much my relatives and family history meant to me. All those cousins, aunts, and uncles I kept talking about only confused her. As we followed Mr. Wright's truck, I filled her in about my ancestors being among the first settlers in the area in the early 1820s and that many of their descendants stayed. This time she listened with fascination because suddenly my family became part of her business.

As we pulled over the hill and turned onto the driveway to the home place, she oohed and aahed at the river valley scene below us while I cringed at the view of the no-longer-existing buildings. I pointed out the lay of the land, the flat river-bottom fields backed by the tree-lined river and bordered on the left by the bluffs and woods. Beyond that, where we couldn't see, was the open pastureland up on the ridge.

"He said he had a hundred acres to work with, so I'm assuming he isn't speaking of the sixty acres in the bottom fields," I said. Then I couldn't help exclaiming, "All those grand buildings gone! And that ugly sore of the pond bank!"

"You've got to get over it," Connie said. "It doesn't look bad to me at all. In fact, I think it's beautiful, or will be when grass grows over everything. Grandiose, that's what it looks like. There's nothing like a pond that size anywhere around here. And what a setting!" She noticed that my back was held stiff and my lips pressed tight together. She held her enthusiasm in check as she continued, "Darrah, there's nothing you can do about it, so try to make the most of it."

"That's almost exactly what my aunt told me."

"A smart woman, your aunt."

Definitely smart. I knew what Aunt Iris would tell me when I told her of the fix I was in. "Darrah girl," she would say, "you've got a dilemma here." Every problem for her was a dilemma. "You can either ruin your chance for a big job and probably make Connie upset with you, or you can make the most of it."

Mr. Wright stopped just after pulling into the space that used to lead up to the house.

"C'mon, partner," Connie said, flipping her long brown hair behind her shoulders. "This is exciting. The biggest job we've ever had. One to die for. Imagine, a hundred acres to landscape!" When I didn't respond as quickly as she wanted, she looked hard at me. "You aren't going to spoil this, are you?" I shook my head. "Good, because I can't do this job alone, and I don't intend to let it get away."

Sometimes Connie treated me like a little sister, or even as if I were her daughter. But to be fair to her, she did this only when I needed a talking-to or when I sulked. Like now. Intellectually, I knew I was being sullen and uncooperative. My attitude could cost us this job. But emotionally, when our two pickups stopped in the scraped bare area where the drive used to be, all I could see were my aging great-grandparents rocking on the front porch with outstretched arms to hug me as I ran up the steps, eager to hear all their stories. And, in the open door to the living room, wearing a printed feed sack apron and grasping a crocheted pot holder in her hand, stood Aunt Iris. I could even smell the mouthwatering aromas of freshly baked bread, fried chicken, and blackberry cobbler.

Instead of that nostalgic picture, I saw the red, raw, pebbly subsoil embankment that blocked out our view of the comforting green line of the woods in the background.

"Darrah!" Connie admonished me again. Her mouth was clamped tight, and she ever so slightly shook her head at me as Mr. Wright walked up to us, unrolling a large survey map of the farm. I read the plea in her eyes and responded to her light pat on my knee.

I shook myself, nodded to her that I would be good, and crawled out of our truck.

"Tell us what you have in mind, Mr. Wright," I said in a thin voice that I hardly recognized as mine. I grabbed a pencil and pad, slapped my floppy work hat on my head to ward off any more freckles popping out on my fair skin, and in every outward sign was ready for business.

"First, call me Moss, Miss Loveland," he said. The corners of his lips turned up just slightly, not smiling, but pleasant.

"Darrah and Connie," I said, indicating our names. My voice was no longer strained.

Connie grinned at me. We were going to nail this job. No sweat. Dilemma or not.

Chapter Three

"As I told you the other day over the phone, Darrah, I have about a hundred acres to work with." Moss pronounced my name with a slightly rolled R, as a Scot would, though there were no other Scottish accents in his speech. "I've rented out the river-bottom fields, and I won't do anything with them. However, I am concerned about the border along the river and stretch of rough land across the river."

I forced myself to listen to him so I could take notes. Since I can write quickly with a sort of self-invented shorthand, it is my job to get everything down. Even though Connie was the one asking questions, and I was obviously busy with my pencil and pad, Moss spoke mostly to me. Connie would ask him something. He would look at her briefly, but finish his answer to me, even though she was closer to him and six inches taller than I am. It was as if he were trying to make me understand, or maybe he was just trying to figure me out.

I was also trying to figure myself out. Being back on the farm for the first time since I was eight opened up memories and sensations I'd forgotten. Instead of being co-owner of the county's only landscaping firm, with a reputation for directness and efficiency, I was a little girl tagging after my older cousins, waiting for Aunt Iris's call for dinner. But the picture was all wrong. There was no imposing rough oak barn built on a bank with its loft full of aromatic hay and its narrow steps leading to the stalls downstairs. In its place was red subsoil and a rock slab where a bulldozer had smoothed out the ground. The pond water was rapidly covering the entire spot.

Instead of an active Gramps telling stories about long ago when he was a young man in the West or Aunt Iris telling about her childhood when the house was built, this self-assured Moss Wright was rattling off how he planned to improve the place. Improve? He, who had obliterated all evidence of the Loveland family era?

Connie gave me a warning poke as I stopped taking notes. She lowered her eyebrows at me and cocked her head toward him to remind me to get with it. Moss was describing the various native plantings he wanted. That was my area of expertise and here I was lagging behind him and Connie saying nothing. Like a pouty child. I did notice that he seemed quite familiar with many plants, calling some by their botanical names. No other client I had worked with did that. I should have been impressed, but I could see only destruction when I looked at him. So I kept my eyes on my notes and let Connie do the talking.

"Darrah knows more about the native plants than I do," Connie said in answer to some question.

"Huh? I'm sorry," I said when they both looked expectantly at me. "I didn't hear what you said."

"I want this entrance section done first to get rid of the bleak look," Moss said. "I'm not sure just what I want to do with this area, whether to sow it to grass or plant native trees. What would you suggest?"

Since no one would ask such a question of a little girl, I reentered the present. Reminding myself that this was a job like any other, I forced myself to be objective. From our vantage point standing on top of the hateful pond bank, we could easily see the few acres in question. A draw coming down from the meadow hill was caught by the embankment. I remembered there used to be a ditch there where Gramps dumped tree limbs and other debris. The U-shaped pond bank intersected the natural draw that continued on the other side of the dam slightly downhill to the flat river-bottom field. The benchland, the area we were discussing, opened up and spread out from the steep wooded hill behind it and sloped to the bottomland. The only level area of the homestead site was where the buildings once stood—the house, the smokehouse, outhouse, chicken house, barn, and silo. Now that was all gouged out to form the five-acre impoundment. Hidden in the rounded embankment was all the good topsoil, including Gramps's daffodils, the old-fashioned well pump, the slatted front gate, and my memories. *"No,"* I could hear Aunt Iris saying, *"no one can bury memories."*

"What do you suggest?" Moss repeated when I continued to ponder.

Repressing my memories, I studied the area professionally. "I think that a combination of grass and trees would be effective. Leave most of the area open with short grasses and then plant occasional groupings of large and understory trees. That would give it a shady, savannah effect. Then in the rougher places, and those where the rocks are exposed, plant glade shrubs, perennial flowers, and forbs. Some ferns would be good."

I studied the area, seeing what I suggested. "The arrangement of the plantings should lead the visitors' eyes up the hill to the bluff and woods behind, while welcoming them to the natural, peaceful spot of the pond environment."

Connie's relief was audible as she let out her breath. The corners of Moss's lips turned up into a definite smile, showing his strong, white teeth.

"That fits my vision perfectly," he said. He removed his cap, ran his fingers through his hair, and replaced the cap, pulling the bill down to his eyes.

"Good," I said. I was working on automatic now, my business demeanor in cruise control. This could be any of the dozens of places we gave estimates on. Moss was just another client to whom I needed to explain my vision of how his place would look. I scanned the area and said with authority and conviction, "Now the first thing we need to do is to get rid of this naked, scarred look." I didn't look at Connie because I knew she would be giving me warning glances that I was back again on dangerous ground.

When Moss nodded in agreement, I continued, ''We need to make the pond a natural part of the total picture instead of a monstrous canyon that swallowed the h . . .''

''Darrah!'' Connie poked me and shook her head. Then she smiled at Moss as a weak apology for me.

I stopped. I was doing so well until I remembered that when his chores were done or after dinner before going back to the fields, Gramps loved to sit on the porch of the house that once stood not far from where we were standing. Right out there, buried in the water in the center of the pond. When I remembered that, the words tumbled out before I could stop them.

Instead of taking offense at my words, Moss laughed and turned to Connie. ''She's pretty feisty, isn't she?'' Connie held up her hands to show that she couldn't control me.

As I stared at the glistening surface of the water, I noticed a few bubbles rising to the surface. Farther out I saw some widening ripples behind what I presumed to be the head of a small animal swimming away from us. Probably a frog. The water level was higher than I'd remembered from my quick look on Monday. I thought that was strange, because it hadn't rained. Also, the water was clearer than I expected it to be in so new a pond.

''You're right, Darrah,'' Moss said. ''It is stripped and unnatural. That's exactly why I've contacted you for help.'' He glanced at Connie to see if he was saying the right things. When she nodded, he continued.

"Your ideas sound great. Go ahead and draw up a detailed plan for this whole area. We'll start on the entrance first."

When I agreed, he asked us to get into his pickup to drive over the rest of the farm. He drove first to the river along the path beside the bottom fields. "I've rented out these fields to Jurgen," Moss said, waving his arm out of his pickup window to encompass the rows of corn ready for picking and the not-quite-as-matured soybeans. "The past owners have taken excellent care of these fields. There is no erosion and the soil is rich and loamy. It's the woods and pastures that have suffered."

Though I didn't try to justify my family's actions, I understood. With no other income, they made their living and raised their families from what the land produced. The bottom fields had to be kept fertile to produce year after year. Likewise, my ancestors needed pasture for their animals. The trees had to go for grass to grow. Without the tree cover, the hills eroded. Being a naturally forested area, scrub trees began to take over when Gramps became too old to keep the sprouts cut down. The Lovelands' tenure on the land was in a different time period from the present. They literally wrested their living from the land. If the land suffered, that was regrettable, but better it suffer than the family starve or lose the land because they weren't able to pay their taxes.

We stopped to inspect the natural row of trees lining the river and protecting the riverbanks.

"Howdy, young feller," said an old-timer who was alone, fishing from the backseat of an aluminum, flat-bottomed boat. He held one homemade paddle that he used occasionally to keep his boat where he wanted it. "And ladies," he said when Connie and I appeared in the path behind Moss Wright.

"Catching anything?" I asked.

For answer, the familiar-looking man leaned over the side of his boat, grabbed a line, and held up a string of bass.

"Wow!" Connie said. "That's good."

The man's toothless grin spread over his face, wrinkling it more than it already was. "I usually get my limit," he said, casting his fly expertly under the canopy of sycamore leaves just to our left. "Well, young Wright, ain't you gonna introduce me to your friends?"

He was Elbow Jurgen who lived up on the highway. I knew I should know him, but it had been several years since I'd seen him. "So this here pretty little lady is ol' Cyrus's little pet," Elbow said to me. "Your great-grandpa was mighty proud of you. You was always a little thing. You still are. No bigger'n a minute."

He winked at Moss, but before he could say anything more, Moss explained our presence. "Darrah and Connie are from Magic Landscaping. They are helping me landscape around the lake. I wanted to show the place to them."

"That's mighty fine. That'd please ol' Cyrus. He had a way with plants. Knew the names of every flower and tree there was, I reckon." He looked at me. "He'd be pleased that someone in the family is interested in the place."

"I haven't been back since Aunt Iris moved off after he died," I said.

Elbow nodded his head. "The buildings kinda went to pot after Cyrus died and Iris sold it. Nobody much took care of the old place after that. Not like that grandson of mine. Darrah, did you notice how he's fixed up my house?" The pride in his eyes was unmistakable.

"I sure did. Aunt Iris commented on it."

"He don't want me to work. Says I've done enough of it in my time and it's his turn now. He's a blessing. I've been retired some dozen years or so. So I don't do much lately but fish and remember the old times. I think lots of ol' Cyrus. A good man. He was quite the storyteller, you know."

"Did he tell you stories, too? I thought he just did that to entertain us kids."

"Naw, he was full of them. He was twenty years or so older'n me. I've got just a couple of years over your Aunt Iris. When he came back from the West, he told me some whoppers. Better'n a dime novel. You betcha." He had reeled in his line and tossed it again. "Come see me," he said as we waved to him before returning to the pickup. "My grandson and his wife are taking real good care of me."

"The grandson is the one farming my fields," Moss explained.

I tried to remember something else I should know about Elbow. I used to see him occasionally when I rode with Gramps. I couldn't remember anything except he had some livestock and a big garden. Maybe he was a teacher, or perhaps the storekeeper? I had a

vague feeling that he held some special position besides being a farmer and a lifelong neighbor.

Moss retraced the route from the river back through
the pond area and without stopping, drove us up the
steep, rocky path to the pasture and woods on the
bluff. It was the very same trail that Gramps used to
take when all of us kids piled into the back of his old
pickup. We used to scream with pleasure, pretending
to be afraid, as we jolted up the steep trail. From our
high vantage point, we used to look down on the shining metal of the barn roof. We could almost see down
inside the concrete silo to the steamy corn ensilage.

As soon as Moss left the area where the buildings
once were, I became completely comfortable with the
surroundings. The thrill of riding on the narrow, almost perpendicular trail brought back the pleasant
feelings I used to have going with Gramps after the
cows. There were no regrets up here. Squeezed on the
seat between Moss and Connie, I looked straight ahead
through the windshield. Everything was much the
same. Moss was as sure of himself in driving up the
hill as Gramps had always been. The trees were bigger, and in the open pasture on top, the grass was more
lush than I remembered. The weed trees—cedars,
hawthorns, and other brush—that were beginning to
take over in Gramps's less-active days were gone.
Thick fescue grass covered the area, though I saw a
few areas of native bluestem and switchgrass that had
survived.

We crossed the level pastureland on top of the bluff
to the woods that covered the hilly, rougher land on
the north side. The farm was nestled in a bend of the

river that flowed on two sides of it. The north-flowing river formed the east boundary where the bottom fields were until it hit the bluff that turned it east. It then made a big half circle that included a couple of other farms until it curved back to the west to create the north edge of the farm. The farm was sort of a bridge, or shortcut, across a big loop of the river. We stopped before we reached this rough wooded land along the river where Moss could no longer drive the truck.

When he turned off his engine and we got out, it was very quiet. None of us said anything as we relished the verdant natural world that was such a contrast to the sterile entrance area. My spirits lifted as I ran from white oak tree to black walnut, pointing out chicory, asters, blazing star, and other fall flowers.

"Oh!" I stopped in a hollow, sinklike depression that was filled with pine trees. Though shortleaf pine is native, this was not a native variety. It was ponderosa pine.

"How could that western pine grow wild here?" Connie asked.

"I've wondered about that, too," Moss said. "I can't explain it."

"I know how," I said, remembering Gramps telling me about planting the big pine tree in his front lawn. "My great-grandfather brought back some plants from his days in Colorado. He loved plants and knew all their names. Probably the reason I majored in horticulture was the interest he instilled in me."

"And the squirrels carried the cones up here?" Connie asked.

"Probably. The young trees spread and naturalized. Isn't that great?"

Moss said, "I've noticed some other unusual plants along the bluff. Did he bring back other plants, too?"

"I think so."

All three of us were excited as Moss and I, in addition to the many plants I recognized, pointed out to Connie the natural geological wonders of the farm. We crossed a natural bridge, and peeked briefly into three different caves, the largest one with a spring flowing from its mouth. We showed Connie one of the small sinkholes and some big rock outcropping.

"This is wonderful," Connie said. "Darrah, how could your family ever let it go?"

"It was hard, but none of my aunts and uncles had the means to buy the others out. Only Aunt Iris was a farmer. Selling it was really the only option. I remember I cried. I'm sure Aunt Iris did, too. If it had been now instead of when I was little, I'd go into debt to buy it."

I could read in Connie's expressions the same thought that I had. I didn't own it, but I now had the opportunity to restore its natural aspects. And Moss was agreeing with every idea I had. I was all business now, dozens of ideas and possibilities running through my mind. "If you want to return the land to native flora," I said to Moss, "I'd suggest getting rid of all this fescue in the pasture and seeding prairie grasses. Good seed is on the market now, including prairie flower seed. You might add more diversity to the varieties of trees. Plant more white oak, hard maple, hickory, and black walnut, for a start. Then we can work on introducing some ferns, forbs . . .''

I could hardly contain myself with the prospects the place presented. And I would be instrumental in making them happen! But I sobered remembering that it wasn't the Loveland farm anymore. I'd be doing it for this interloper to our county. So what? At least he wasn't planning to raze the woods as so many land buyers did by bulldozing off all the hillsides to make more pasture. He was doing the opposite.

Connie's happy face was all the encouragement I needed. We would accept this job that would assure us a steady income this winter and promise of work for months to come.

"We'll need to take some measurements. We could have a tentative overall plan and estimate ready next week, in addition to a detailed plan for the entrance." I turned to Connie to get her approval. She nodded.

"Good," Moss said, a big grin on his face. "When you're ready, give my secretary a call to set up an appointment." He handed me his card.

All the way back to town Connie didn't stop talking about Moss Wright and *his* place. "It's like the answer to a prayer. It makes our spot plantings and pruning jobs seem like child's play."

"Yeah." I was grinning happily.

"It'll cost him a bundle. Do you think he's good for it?"

"I don't know anything about him."

"We better do some checking before we invest too much time in it."

I agreed. Connie was the business brains of our partnership. Collecting our money was sometimes hard to do. Because she got burned a couple of times with nonpaying clients when we first started out, she checked out new customers. However, having the money did not always mean that people paid us right away. Some of our hardest bill collecting was from wealthy people.

"He seemed honest," Connie said. "At least he had money to buy the place and tear down the buildings."

I groaned.

"Oh, Darrah, get off of that."

"I'll try."

We drove for a couple of miles in silence, each thinking about the job.

"He wasn't wearing a wedding ring," Connie said, flipping her hair behind her shoulders. She looked steadily at me to see my reaction.

I didn't react, but continued driving, my eyes straight ahead on the highway. Aunt Iris had also noticed his lack of a ring.

"Plus, he's a looker," Connie said.

I laughed at her. "Sounds like you're going to check out more than his finances."

"I may. But there's really no reason to."

"Why?" This answer surprised me. Connie loved to flirt. She always had three dates to my one. She seemed to have a sixth sense when it came to men—knowing which ones were uninvolved and which were interested in her.

"Because, my dear Darrah, he barely looked at me the whole time we were with him. He never took his eyes off of you, even when you were insulting him or pouting like a spoiled kid."

"Aw, you're exaggerating."

"No, I'm not. And another reason I don't need to 'investigate' him is that I know he is single and uninvolved."

"Now how do you know that?"

"I just do. I'm rarely wrong."

I had to admit she was right. She was never mistaken about people. I also noticed that he looked at me a lot, but I thought it was because he was hiring me to do a big job. It was natural for him to check me out. This job would cost him many thousands of dollars. Or he might have felt guilty about the buildings and kept watching me to gauge my reactions. Aunt Iris's sharp words to him on Monday definitely disconcerted him, even though we had no idea then that he was the one who had torn down the buildings. And then today again, I said several things right out to show how much I disapproved of what he had done.

"Well, I'm not interested in *him*."

"Yeah, yeah!" Connie teased me.

"No way. I'll do this job because it means so much to our business, but that is the end of it. And I can tell you that working there in the house area will be very difficult for me. Every minute all I will think of is that this man destroyed my heritage. I'm not sure that I can even be civil to him all the time."

Connie shook her head. She had no way of understanding my feelings or how empty I felt with the homestead gone. "Houses are torn down all the time to create something new," she said. "What's the big deal?"

It was a humongous deal to me. And to all my relatives. Especially Aunt Iris. My black mood returned. How could I tell Aunt Iris that I was now aiding and abetting the enemy? Perhaps an even harder job than working in the entrance area would be handling my own feelings of guilt when I told her I was doing it.

So I wouldn't tell her. I knew I couldn't do that. I always talked with her about our jobs. She would never forgive me if I didn't tell her in detail all about this one.

"I wonder why he tore down the buildings," Connie said. "I almost asked him several times, but decided I better not. I was afraid of setting you off."

"I don't want to know," I lied, because I did want to know, but was worried that the reason would upset me more—just as Connie feared.

Connie began chatting about our plans. Being the organized one, she was already jotting down things we had to do, and adding up some estimates, exclaiming at our good fortune in landing this job. Her enthusiasm infected me. Designing and landscaping a hundred acres of Ozark land!

"I sure hope he's loaded," I said, laughing, "for if he is, we'll make that farm a showcase for the entire state."

"All right!" Connie patted me on the shoulder as we turned into our place of business.

"Magic Landscaping." I read aloud the sign Connie had painted and installed by our driveway. It *was* magical, the whole business—our neat little office and the greenhouses behind it. The rows of trees and shrubs and the potting boxes of flowering plants and ferns neatly displayed to one side, all proved our mission and our motto, "The magic of landscaping makes the home and the world a better place."

Connie and I both believed our motto. With creative design and with natural and human assets, we helped shape a beautiful and healthful environment. *Now,* I reasoned, *we have an opportunity to do it on a grand scale. And one that won't hurt our pocketbooks, either.*

Chapter Four

Before I could figure out how I was going to tell Aunt Iris about Moss Wright's hiring us, she called me. She had already heard about it from her cousin Abby who knew all the family news. The one and only time we ever scooped her was learning first about the destruction of the farm buildings. Aunt Iris had already learned that the man who almost ran into us was the new owner of the Loveland farm, and more than that, she knew that I was consorting with the enemy. But she wasn't upset at all that I agreed to landscape the farm.

"Good for you," she said almost gleefully, as if Moss Wright's paying me all that money was his just deserts. I was greatly relieved. But I should have known she would see the broader view. Always the realist, she accepted things the way they were without making herself miserable about things that couldn't be changed. "I'm glad you've put aside your aversion to him and what he did."

"But I haven't! I could hardly stand to be there on that horrid pond bank and see what he did. It looks even worse close up." Since my voice was stretching thin and high in my outrage, I took a couple of deep breaths. "But I just couldn't turn down such a big job. Connie and I . . ."

"Of course, Darrah girl. Of course, you had to take the job. I do know how you feel, but no sense getting into a huff about it. It'll work out, you'll see. Just think of what you can do for the farm. You have the opportunity to do what all the generations of Lovelands before you couldn't do. You can do what's best for the land without having to support a family from what it produces. More than that, you will get paid royally for it. Just think, when you finish, the farm will be better off than it has ever been since the first Loveland started chopping down the trees."

"How can that be? The house is gone. And that wonderful barn!"

"Buildings come and go. The land, Darrah girl, the land. That's what's important. The early Lovelands, up to my father's time, cut down most of the good trees to make fields and pastures, as well as for lumber and firewood. Because of the erosion, the river is choking up with gravel. We even plowed up the natural prairie grasses in the bluff pasture to sow that awful fescue."

"But the house."

"Papa would agree with me that houses aren't permanent. The land is. He was the first Loveland to do anything about reversing the trend of exploiting the land. He made a small effort to improve it by planting trees in the rough places and controlling some erosion. Now you have a chance to make a big difference. Papa would like that.''

"Maybe."

"No maybe about it."

"Improving the land was what convinced me to take the job. I've thought of nothing else since Connie and I were there yesterday. I have many ideas worked out in my head. I'm sketching them from the information we got. Connie is inventorying the plants we'll need and figuring up an estimate.''

"Good."

"Money doesn't seem to be a problem with this guy. Not once did he even mention costs other than for us to prepare an estimate for him. It's the biggest job we've ever had.'' In spite of my determination to stay negative, my voice showed enthusiasm.

"Sounds like it's not all bad."

"*If* the guy is good for it. He wants us to do the entrance area first—you know, the seven or eight acres around that pond. Even that area will cost plenty.''

"Oh, he's good for it," Aunt Iris said in her I-know-I-am-right tone. Cousin Abby had beat Connie in getting the goods on Moss Wright.

"Okay, then tell me."

"Young Wright is not related to any of the Wrights in the county. He's from the East somewhere, Pennsylvania or New York, and was transferred here about a year ago to head up the Moss Industries plant in

Timberton. He comes from big money. Grandson, I think Abby said, of the founder.''

Of course! I thought I should know who he was. When the Moss plant came to town there was a big hullabaloo. Quite a coup for our town, as it hired five hundred people right away. Connie and I even did a spot planting around the employees' entrance. We worked with one of the underlings, never seeing the main boss.

''He likes to keep a low profile,'' Aunt Iris continued. ''It's no wonder that we didn't recognize him the other day or that you didn't know his name. He lets his promotion staff handle all the contacts with the public.''

I laughed at how thorough her information was. ''Did Abby tell you anything more?''

''Oh, yes.'' She chuckled. ''He is thirty years old, an only child of deceased parents, and''—she paused for me to appreciate her next bit of information—''he isn't married.'' I could imagine the smug look on her face that her first impression of him in the farm driveway was correct.

Just before she hung up, I said, ''We ran into Elbow Jurgen fishing down on the river. His grandson lives with him and fixed up his house. He's the one who farms the bottom fields.''

''I'm glad to hear that. Elbow and Papa were always good buddies. When Elbow was just a kid, he used to hang around our place a lot. I've got to go now.''

For the next few days Connie and I hurried through our scheduled jobs. We worked late into the night on Wright's plans. Connie drove back to the farm for some more accurate and detailed measurements and photographs, such as where the pond's waterline would be when full and the natural fall of the ground from the overflow at the spillway. She came back more excited about the job than before.

"You wouldn't believe how quickly the pond is filling," she said after her first trip. "With so much water, it's too big to be a called a pond. It's a lake." There was wonder in her voice. "And the water is already deep and very clear."

I was surprised that the one-inch rain we had over the weekend could add so much water and especially that it would clear up so quickly. But then I realized that the pond's watershed was probably thirty acres of wooded or grassy land—all the area from the ridge road and the steep meadow where we stopped to get the view of the farm.

Knowing my aversion to the pond, she studied me to see how I reacted to her enthusiasm. "With all that water," she said hesitantly, "it doesn't look so raw. It'll really be beauti—"

"Okay, okay," I interrupted her, "you don't need to coddle me. It's our job to make it beautiful. So let's get to it." She grinned at me. I was coming along.

As promised, by the next week we had the detailed drawings and an estimate ready for the entrance area around the pond, and less-detailed overall plans for the bluff and pasture areas. We met Moss in the conference room next to his office, where he greeted us enthusiastically. I tried not to be impressed by his office complex or the three levels of staff people we checked through to get to him. Our little barn-turned-office at

Magic Landscaping would fit into the Moss Industries conference room alone.

Though dressed in a stylish tan business suit and tie, Moss behaved like a little boy expecting his first bicycle. He shook hands with both of us, his face wreathed in full-blown smiles, not the barely turned-up corners of his lips as before. "You have them ready so soon?" Though he glanced at Connie occasionally, he concentrated most of his attention toward me.

"Yes, we said we'd have them ready in a week," I said. We were off to a good start. Apparently he wasn't used to such promptness.

He reached out to take the portfolio of papers that Connie had carefully arranged in order.

"Perhaps we should explain them a bit," I said as Connie spread them out on the big conference table.

He nodded and waited impatiently until she finished. Then without saying anything and moving around the table, he carefully studied each sheet of the detailed plans for the entrance, methodically going over every inch of the drawings and checking the cost estimates. Connie and I watched his face anxiously for any sign of his thoughts. At times his eyebrows contracted as he studied some area, but when he understood my symbols, his forehead smoothed out and he looked up at me and nodded slightly. When he picked up the big sketch showing what the whole entrance area would look like when completed, he moved his head from side to side just slightly, as if amazed. Though he didn't vocalize it, I saw his lips form a "Wow."

"Good," he said, carefully stacking the entrance

plans on the table to his right. "You must have read my mind. This gives exactly the look and feel that I wanted. You've shown that you can make my ideas come true." Then for the first time since greeting her, he addressed Connie. "It'll be awesome, won't it?"

Connie grinned and flipped her hair over her shoulder. "Of course. We're magic."

"That you are." He picked up the sketches and estimates for the rest of the farm. After scanning them quickly, he asked to keep them to study at his leisure. He pulled out his personal checkbook and referring back to Connie's neat row of figures on the entrance estimates, asked, "I assume you require half now and the rest when completed?"

Connie gulped. Usually we had to ask clients for starting money and most of the time they weren't willing to pay until the job was done. We were anticipating having to borrow from the bank to pay our workers and get the supplies and hundreds of plants we listed.

I showed no reaction as I answered him. "Yes, that is our usual practice. Less the hundred dollars you paid for the estimates."

He wrote out a check right then, ripped it off, and handed it to me. I thrilled inwardly at the figure, which was the largest amount we'd ever received at one time.

"Darrah," Moss said, slipping his checkbook into his inside jacket pocket, "I'm sure that you will agree with me that the place will be better without the old buildings." His smile was again the just-turned-up corners of his mouth, as if he was not sure of my reaction.

My elation disappeared, drowned in the waves of memories surfacing by his mention of the buildings. In spite of Aunt Iris's and Connie's advice to me, my bitterness returned. Merely by holding Moss's check, I felt that I was a traitor to Gramps.

I jumped up, dropping my portfolio case and knocking my purse onto the floor. I'm sure the flush in my face was red enough to hide my freckles. I stood as tall as my five-foot-one body could reach. "How can you say . . ."

Connie grabbed the check from my hands before I mutilated it, and put her hand on my arm. She gave me a determined look, her stern mothering look that demanded I behave.

I took hold of myself and cleared my throat to speak in my normal voice. "We hoped you would like our plans. We can start work right away, as we have many of the plants needed. We will have to order the big trees, but we will have them in about a week. We'll start first with the tractor work, smoothing out and contouring the area around some exposed rocks to get ready for the topsoil."

"Great," Moss said, shooting a glance at Connie that seemed to indicate a silent conspiracy between them to control me and convince me about the buildings.

Moss accompanied us out of the room and shook our hands—mine last. "I'm truly sorry about the buildings," he said to me. "I didn't know they were of such value to your family. They were in bad repair from years of neglect, and they were not located where I might later want to build." He paused. "That location was the best place on the farm to build a lake. I did hate to lose that wonderful pine and the maple trees.'' When I didn't say anything, he added almost boyishly, ''The farm is so wonderful that I just want to make it even better.''

Yeah, I thought. *Make a place better by tearing down its lifeblood?*

When I still made no response, Connie said, ''Until a couple of weeks ago, she hadn't been back to the farm since she was eight.'' With the check safely stashed in her billfold and with me under control, she probably felt she should explain my rudeness. At least she filled the embarrassing pause.

''I understand,'' Moss said. ''Seeing the lake with no warning like that must have been quite a shock. I got a taste of her reaction myself.''

They were discussing me as if I either wasn't there or was a child too young to understand adult conversation.

I couldn't take that anymore. ''Let's go, Connie.'' I pulled her to the door and made myself smile brightly at Moss. ''Good day, Mr. Wright. I trust you will be at the farm some of the time while we are working?''

''Of course. As much as I can spare from here.'' He spread out his hands to indicate his work at Moss Industries.

Connie scolded me for my behavior as we drove first to the drive-up window at the bank to deposit the check and then the two miles out to our nursery. But her usual jovial spirit returned. In spite of my behavior, we had nailed the job; the check was safely in the bank.

"He really likes you, Darrah. Did you notice how he took your rudeness? Getting that kind of treatment, anyone else would tell us to get lost."

"Yeah, yeah, I know. I'm sorry. It won't happen again."

The next day our workers hauled our heavy dirt-moving equipment to the farm. During our busy season we have two crews. We sent one crew to finish our other jobs, while Carl and Allen followed us in the big truck to begin the Wright job. While I instructed the guys what to do, Connie was studying the pond. I joined her.

I had to admit that the scene didn't look as bare as before. Much of the red subsoil was now hidden by water. The banks still gave off the raw look, but the truckloads of topsoil we ordered would soon cover them. Just then the first dump truck piled high with rich, black soil crept down the rough driveway from the ridge.

I turned my attention to the pond's water level. No way, I thought, could that much water have accumulated with the one rain we'd had since Aunt Iris and I first saw it. Connie was right. This was a lake. Four or five acres qualifies as more than a pond. We walked around the perimeter of the lake. A frog leaped into the water with a splash. The ripples from his dive circled out on the clear surface. Water spiders scurried around the edges. Several cardinals flew up when we got near them and landed across the water on an exposed boulder. A flock of Canada geese circled overhead and then continued on south. The pond was beginning to live.

On the southern bank where the natural ditchlike draw once cut across the slope leading to the bottom fields, I paused to study the water surface. Though not crystal clear like a spring, the water was much less murky than water in a newly formed lake should be. Its quality was more like that of the river just below the big spring.

A spring feeding the lake would explain not only the water condition, but why it was filling up so quickly. But I didn't remember any spring. The driveway through the gate used to go over the ditch right under where I was standing. Gramps had even installed a metal whistle when he got tired of fixing up the drive after every big rain. When we were kids he used to caution us to stay away from the ditch. By my time the ditch was almost filled in with tree branches and washed-in dirt and gravel.

Gramps used to say, "Now, listen here. You young'uns keep away from that there ditch. They's things in there that could hurt you if you fell in."

"You could break your leg," Aunt Iris added.

I chuckled as I remembered their warnings. Now the spot was under many feet of water. Kids really *could* hurt themselves if they fell in there and didn't know how to swim.

To get my bearings, I glanced toward the fencerow separating the steep meadow from the entrance area. I followed an imaginary waterline in the lake where the ditch used to be. My landscaping plans eliminated the old ditch where it left the lake bank by smoothing out the soil. With our tractor blade and backhoe, Carl was already leveling all remnants of the ditch. The new runoff from the lake came out north of that. Using the natural contours of the slope, my plan created a curving path for the spillway to run down to the fence line of the bottom fields. Moss especially liked my idea of a rustic bridge to take the driveway over the spillway.

The enigma of the high-water level puzzled me. At noon break, I went to the pickup to call Aunt Iris on my cell phone.

"I had almost forgotten about it," Iris said, "but, yes, there used to be a spring there. I don't remember it so much as remember hearing about it. Way back when the first Lovelands settled there in the early 1800s, that spring was their water source. And it continued to be for many years. I think it was my father who dug the first well. I don't know how much flow the spring had. I sort of remember that there was a hollowed-out place lined with rocks that held the water."

"What happened to the spring?"

"By my time it had petered out. Lots of springs dried up after the trees were all cut down. Or it may have put out so little water that it was just a wet place."

"And it would have been a nuisance?"

"Probably. We used that ditch for dumping our trash."

"Yeah, I even remember Gramps warning us not to go near it."

"It was something he always worried about way

before your time, even with us kids." She chuckled. "He was very strict about it. I'd forgotten that. Once he punished Arnie and me for messing around down there. We all learned to stay away from it."

"Well, that was smart, for springwater seeping in could make a dangerous place for kids. Besides attracting snakes!"

So a spring explained the good lake water and why it was filling so rapidly. In spite of myself, I became excited. Connie and I climbed the bank again to see if we could spot where the spring came out. Just then Moss drove up in his pickup. Connie waved to him to join us on the bank. He was dressed again in his jeans, T-shirt, cap, and work shoes.

"The water is filling up even faster than I thought," he said.

"My aunt just told me on the phone there used to be a spring here. I didn't know about it. I guess you discovered it while bulldozing."

"Yes, I did. Didn't I tell you about it?" We shook our heads. "I suppose I assumed you knew about it since you put into your plans the little stream from the spillway. I was here the day the machines dug down and uncovered the spring. I told them to clean up around its opening, but not to ruin it. We changed the shape of the lake to take advantage of the spring."

"A spring-fed lake!" Connie said. "That's even better yet."

"That's what I thought," Moss said. "I couldn't believe my luck. We dug down a bit more and uncovered a rock ledge. I guess it was the original outlet of the spring, because water started flowing out much faster. It isn't a gushing spring, but it has a pretty good output. It won't take many more days for the lake to fill up. Then your little stream will have a steady flow of water.''

I mentally added to my plans some water plants like watercress and some decorative reeds. I hadn't visualized a continually running stream. I thought of a few other enhancements to the plan to take advantage of the constant water flow.

Connie didn't understand. ''It doesn't make sense. How could a dried-up spring suddenly start flowing?''

''The water was there all along, underground,'' I explained, ''but it didn't surface. Like water that we tap by digging a well. Only this water is closer to the surface. With a lot of silt washing in and the flow diminishing with the destruction of the forests, the water probably went underground somewhere, maybe coming out in the river.''

Moss pointed out to us the exact spot in the lake. Though the view was hazy through the water which was still tainted by the runoff and raw dirt, we could make out a ledge of gray limestone slabs protruding from the otherwise red bottom.

''The spring isn't in the deepest place,'' Moss said. ''When we discovered it, we didn't want to excavate it for fear of destroying it. We didn't disturb the rocks where it emerged, but sloped the lake bottom down from there to get the depth I wanted.'' He pointed to a spot in the lake closer to us and a bit south and east of the spring. There the water was too clouded to see all the way to the bottom. ''That's the deepest section.

When the lake fills and the particles in the water precipitate out, we should be able to see the bottom."

"How deep down is the spring?" Connie asked. I knew exactly what she was thinking. This would be a good place to keep up with our scuba diving. We hadn't done much lately; we needed to dive regularly to keep in shape.

"When the lake fills completely, the spring will be under about fifteen feet of water. The deepest place in the lake should be about twenty-five feet."

"Wow!" I was amazed, and intrigued. Imagine scuba diving within sight of Gramps's front porch. Without the usual sinking feeling I experienced when I looked at the watery spot where the house once stood, I let my eyes move over the water surface. The porch was about two hundred feet north of the ditch. I pinpointed the watery spot.

"It would be fun to scuba dive and explore the spring close up," I said. I thought I could see an opening in the rock ledge of the spring.

"Do you scuba dive?" Moss asked, his eyes lighting up.

"Yes, Connie and I both do. We used to do quite a bit of it when we were in the university. We've done some here in the county, but not as much as we'd like."

"That's great." His little-boy enthusiasm was in his voice. "I'm learning. I just received my open-water diver certification. One of the reasons I built this lake was to have a place to practice and keep in shape. I thought it would be much more fun than using a swimming pool, and more convenient than the river."

I was learning that Moss and I had several interests in common. I looked at him with a touch of eagerness. "Then we should dive together sometime." As soon as the words were out, I regretted them. I couldn't believe that I said that. I had actually invited him to do something with me in a nonbusiness venture.

"I'd love that," he said quickly, as if he feared I would retract my invitation. "Where and when?"

Since I'd gotten myself into more than I bargained for, I figured I might as well take advantage of it to learn more about my family's history. "What about right here in the lake? At the rate it's filling, it will be full in a few days. I'd like to see the spring close up."

"Good idea," Connie said. "It's hard to see the details from here. Down there you can study those rock formations around it. What are they like?"

"And how big is the opening?" I asked.

Moss said, "The spring comes out between two horizontal rock shelves. The opening varies along its length, but in the widest place it is probably two feet high and three to four feet wide." He held out his hands to show us the formation as he talked.

"Big enough for me to get inside with diving equipment?" I asked. We were all getting excited.

"You probably could. You're small enough. It wouldn't be safe for me. Or for Connie. We're too big."

"Did you go in when you first discovered the opening?" Connie asked.

"No. I never even thought of crawling inside. It was just a yucky, muddy hole. But without an air tank on my back, there was room enough that I could have wormed my way in.''

"Did you look inside?" I asked.

"Not really. It was layered with dirt from the bull-dozers. It wasn't very inviting. And there was no reason to. It was dark inside and I didn't have a light. Since then the flow of the spring and the lake water has cleaned it up."

"Then it will be fun to be the first people to see what it's like inside."

Moss was catching our enthusiasm. "Yes, it would." He studied the water level and the bubbles breaking on the surface. "We don't have to wait until the lake completely fills. There is enough water now. What about this Saturday?"

Connie and I looked at each other and nodded.

"About nine then. I'll meet you here."

Chapter Five

Moss and I dived to within twelve feet of the spring opening. Since we didn't want to stir up any silt from the bottom to obscure our vision, we adjusted our buoyancy controls to hover on a level with the spring. Though visibility was not as clear as in a swimming pool, we could see quite well through our masks.

The rock ledges of the spring were just as Moss had described them—two horizontal slabs extending several feet on either side of a slitted opening. Chips and gouges on the rocks from the bulldozer blade were still fresh, as was some dirt that settled on the rocks.

It was eerie, being suspended in water at eye level with the spot in the ditch that Gramps warned us to avoid. My scuba diving in that exact spot would be unthinkable to him, even more incredible than some of the exciting tales he used to tell. His tales were about climbing mountain heights, not diving down into the depths of lakes.

For a few minutes Moss and I hovered, enjoying the weightlessness and the extraordinary sights, sounds, and other sensations of diving. Though he obviously knew diving procedures, Moss held back, awaiting my lead to move closer. This was my dive since I was the one interested in exploring the spring. I remained still, experiencing the thrill of being underwater and convincing my mind that I truly was diving in a former hillside. I studied the spring opening to spot the clean springwater and to notice how it flowed into the murkier lake water. Slowly I swam closer, followed by Moss, whose hooded head was on my left side at about my waist.

Our wet suits protected us from the change in temperature as we moved from the warm lake water to the cooler springwater discharging from the opening.

From the lower slab of rock, the dozer had excavated the ground, exposing a small bluff that extended down about ten more feet. From there the lake bottom gradually leveled out to the lowest depth. As we hovered upright side by side at eye level to the opening, bubbles of air from us danced toward the surface where Connie watched from Moss's rowboat. In the natural light, we couldn't see beyond a few inches into the inky depths of the little spring cave.

I pointed to the opening and signaled that I was going in. Moss responded with his thumb and forefinger together in an okay sign. We had already agreed that I would enter the cave if the opening was big enough. Then he flattened out his hand and moved it up and down slightly. "Take it easy," his signal meant.

I nodded and signaled "Okay." Holding my underwater light in front of me, I swam slowly right up to the opening. Uncanny! Not only was there all this impounded water in Gramps's house frontage, but also a miniature bluff spewing out a never-ending stream of crystal water. I had explored underwater caves before, but the thrill during those times was nothing like this. This magic underwater world, superimposed onto the Lovelands' stolid Ozark self-sufficient farm, sent shivers all through me. I kept reminding myself I wasn't in some fairy wonderland.

As I stuck my head inside, I scanned the area with my light beam. As I suspected, the passage opened up. When I entered the cave, small as I was, there would be room for me to maneuver, even to turn around, though not enough room for two of us. I signaled that information to Moss. Carefully propelling myself forward with my fins and feeling above me with my left hand to gauge the height of the ceiling so not to strike it with my scuba tank, I slowly eased my shoulders inside. There was no room to spare. As I paused to study the interior more carefully before going in farther, I couldn't help visualizing the rear view of me that Moss got—my fin-covered feet, and my legs and hips encased in a bright red wet suit. Not my best angle.

Though the bulldozer had swept clean everything at the spring entrance, inside my light picked up a jumble of items behind a log that was rotten and mired in the debris on the clay floor.

Being underwater is like no other sensation I've ever experienced. It gives bodily freedom, like flying must feel to birds or the relief from gravity astronauts experience in space. But entering into an underwater closed-in area, like this little cave, is the antithesis of freedom. It is worse than the confinement and restriction of a single jail cell. More like a coffin. It is frightening to some people and because of the extra danger involved, divers take special training before entering such places.

Out in the open water I can see the natural daylight from above and know that I am free to ascend at any time. Up there on the surface are people watching me, ready to help at any sign of the slightest problem. Not so in an underwater cave. If in trouble, I am trapped in solid rock many feet under water with only a few minutes of air. I am unable to simply ascend, but must first find my way out through the narrow channel opening. And my buddies can't see if I am in trouble.

I had explored underwater caves a few times while training. Not being bothered by claustrophobia, I thrived on the extra hint of danger. Not Connie. Since she was uncomfortable in any cave, she opted to sit this dive out.

Maintaining neutral buoyancy as I was lying prone in the opening, I wormed my way a few inches farther into the cave until the crumbling end of the log partially blocked my way. My legs were the only parts of me that were still outside.

Before moving the log aside, I shined my light over the floor near the log. I recognized the remains of a two-gallon bucket full of ashes, a rusty iron skillet, an old plow point, a bent wheel from some toy, and other discarded items that probably were dumped in the cave opening from Gramps's time. The eerie sensation returned full force. Encased in this watery grave were long-forgotten relics of my early childhood. They brought back the safety of Granny's arms shielding me from all danger. I could sense the warmth of Gramps's smile. In spite of being in this watery environment, I was on their land. I had the feeling that both were still protecting me, just as my wet suit was doing in the fifty-six-degree temperature of the springwater. In this liquid world my imagination ruled.

Careful not to cloud the water with the layers of rotted material around the log that was blocking my way, I reached out my left hand to ease it aside. A piece crumbled off at my touch.

Suddenly the far end of the log broke away and moved on its own as if it knew Gramps needed it to start his fire on this cool September day. For a second I stared at the moving log, stunned at the reality of my fantasy. But I was not imagining the movement. I gasped as the end of the log materialized into a huge, brown turtle, an alligator snapping turtle at least fifteen inches long. The hooked beak on its mouth was opening and closing as its head, protruding out of the accordionlike, loose skin of its neck, swung from side to side. Fleshy projections stuck out of its skin, making it even more horrifying.

For a moment the pupils in the bulging orbs above its beak stared at me. It was probably as startled as I was. And it was undoubtedly frightened since I blocked its exit. It rose from the log and started swimming toward me in what seemed slow motion. Its short, fat legs that ended in sharp talons on the feet moved it through the water.

In panic I dropped my light and frantically clawed the cave floor under me to find something solid to push my upper body back out of the cave. Visibility decreased as I disturbed the years of accumulation on the floor. Even as silt, hunks of wood, and debris floated before my mask, I could still see the angry turtle swimming straight toward my head, its wide mouth snapping continually. As I backed out, my tank scraped against the ceiling, giving a dull thud. My flaying arms struck the rocks on either side of me. I forgot my training, which was to take slow, deep breaths regularly. I held my breath. Just like the dinosaurs in *Jurassic Park*, the beast was eye to eye with me, its ugly mouth opening and closing as it tried to bite my mask, my regulator, or anything it could snap. I threw my right arm up to protect my head, while with the other hand, I grabbed the rough rock surface to push myself out. My whole body was in motion, warding off the turtle and trying to retreat. No longer holding my breath, I gasped in short, shallow, soblike moans.

When the turtle was only inches from my mask, I felt Moss's strong hands grabbing one ankle. Realizing what he was doing, I quit kicking so he could grasp the other leg. With a wrench, he jerked me backward. My tank thudded against the rock ceiling and my left hand scraped against the side. When my head was completely free of the cave, he tugged me away from the spring just as the irate turtle cleared the opening. No longer caged in, it gave us only a passing glance and swam north toward the water's edge. We lost sight of it.

Still holding me with one hand, Moss signaled, "Are you okay?"

I nodded.

We heard the slap of the paddle of the small boat above us as Connie maneuvered it to be at the best location to help. She had seen the disturbance below, but the ensuing struggle that stirred up the sediment obscured her view of what was happening.

I pointed my thumb up, indicating we should ascend.

Moss shook his head when he noticed the unusual amount of bubbles spewing out of my regulator. He held up his hand, signaling, "Stop and rest."

Of course he was right. My close encounter and struggle made me forget the basic rules of steady breathing while diving. I took long, slow breaths for a few minutes to recover. Not only did Moss stay close to me, but he held on to my arm to keep me from floating away. The pressure of his touch made me feel safe. He turned out to be an excellent diving buddy. I patted his arm in response.

"Okay," I signaled when my breathing and my heartbeat returned to normal.

Side by side, his hand still on my arm, we surfaced and quickly climbed into the boat with Connie. I hugged Moss in my delight in being safe and to thank him for saving me. Grinning, he returned the hug.

While we were busy with the hugs, an agitated Connie kept demanding to be told what had happened. When I didn't answer immediately, she turned to

Moss. "Is Darrah all right? I knew she shouldn't enter that cave."

"I think she's okay."

"I'm fine."

"She's just shaken up," Moss said.

"What happened down there?" Connie asked.

"She disturbed a snapping turtle."

"An *alligator* snapping turtle." I wanted them to know it wasn't a little box turtle. "The largest fresh-water turtle in *the world*."

Connie was as impressed as I wanted her to be. I loved being able to tell her about the Ozarks. I could tell that Moss was likewise impressed.

We searched the water surface to see if we could see where the turtle went. Following a line of ripples to its point, I spotted the eyes and hooked beak, the only part of the reptile that was visible above the water. It was almost at the north shore. I pointed. "See? There it goes."

Connie shook her head in dismay at how this dive had turned out. It was supposed to be an elementary dive into a new, not-yet-filled lake where no depth was over twenty feet. What could go wrong? Before Moss and I dived, we had agreed that I would go into the spring if I thought there was enough room, but even if I found a cave passage big enough for me, I wouldn't go beyond the "Twilight Zone"—the area where I could see natural light from the opening. Later we might explore farther, depending on what we found.

All three of us watched the turtle's head become its complete body as it emerged and crawled out of the water. Even from that distance we could see how big it was. "That is a big sucker," Moss said. "I didn't get a good look at him down there. I was too busy pulling you out."

"Try eye to eye with him and you'll believe how big he is," I said. "I've never seen one so big. When I was a kid, we sometimes saw them in the slough or backwaters of the river."

"Didn't they scare you as a child?" Connie asked.

"No. Gramps said if you don't disturb them, they won't hurt you. But sometimes one of my boy cousins would pester one. I always kept a safe distance away."

"Did your great-grandfather know about animals as well as plants?" Moss asked.

"Oh yes. Today we'd call him an environmentalist. He wouldn't let my older cousins shoot the turtles just for target practice as some boys did. He said turtles have as much right to live here as we did. He believed that they had a place in the scheme of nature."

"Well, you certainly disturbed this one," Connie said, as the turtle crawled down the hill. "I don't believe I want to test his theory out on that monster."

We watched the turtle. It moved with more speed than I thought possible. When it reached the bottom fields, it disappeared into the rows of dried cornstalks.

"Where's it going?" Connie asked.

"Back to the river," I said. "He must have been scouting out this pond for a possible new home."

"I bet he doesn't come back!" Moss said.

"I hope not," Connie said. I knew her strong dislike of reptiles of any kind. She would not relish working where one frequented.

"You fouled up his newly found home." Moss gave me his full-blown smile that enhanced his good looks.

"Turtles have to breathe," Connie said. "How could he live down in that cave?"

"They can stay underwater for long periods. They come up for air occasionally," I said. "This one was probably ready to get a breath and that was the reason he was so belligerent. Normally they aren't."

I felt no results from my scare. My hand was bleeding slightly from the scratch, but it wasn't serious. We found no cuts in my wet suit and my tank seemed unhurt, except for a nick on its surface.

"Thanks for pulling me out, Moss."

"That's what a diving buddy is for," he said. "But I've never had to rescue anyone before. Did I do it right?"

"You did good. How'd you know I was in trouble?"

"Your feet were thrashing like mad. I even had trouble grabbing one."

"I could see that from up here in the boat," Connie said. "I was about to dive, when I saw Moss pull you out. Then all your exertions clouded up the water so that I couldn't see how you were." She shook her head. "It was a bad idea to go into that cave."

"I'm going back," I said. "As soon as the water clears up, I'm going down again."

"You're crazy," Connie said. "I won't go with you. No telling what else is in that cave."

"I'll go with you again," Moss said, so quietly that I barely heard him. He was looking over the side of the boat. Already the rocky opening was becoming visible again. "We didn't finish, did we?" he asked me in a louder voice.

"No. I'm more curious than ever. I'd like to see what else my great-grandfather dumped in there. Besides, I left my light in the cave. It's a good one that I don't want to lose."

"You really shouldn't dive again," Connie said.

"I'll be okay. There is enough space inside and I can get in and out without any danger."

"Yeah," Connie said, "maybe another turtle, or worse—water snakes!"

"Not likely now after all that commotion," Moss said. "This would be a good time to return before some other animal takes up housekeeping there. We can soon dive again. Most of what you and Mr. Turtle stirred up was big stuff. It's already settling, and the current from the spring is moving it away."

"What did you see inside the cave?" Connie asked.

I visualized what my light had revealed in the brief time I was there. "Nothing special, really. The cave opens up into a little chamber about six by six feet. Then it narrows. I don't think it's big enough for me to go back any farther. And being newly flooded makes this one different from the other underwater caves I've been in."

"Was there anything unusual there?"

"Not that I saw. There was an old bucket that I'm sure was one of Gramps's that he used to collect his ashes from the wood stove."

"How'd it get in there?" Connie asked.

"He may have discarded it in there as well as all

the other junk I saw to fill it up,'' Moss said. ''Didn't you say, Darrah, that he thought the spring was dangerous?''

''Yes.''

''Probably one reason was the threat from all that broken and rusty metal that could cut children's feet.'' He looked over the side of the boat. The water was once again clear. ''Are you ready?'' I nodded. ''Then let's dive again.''

On the second dive I entered the cave all the way. I retrieved my light and was able to bypass the log without disturbing it further. The turtle's and my actions in escaping the first time moved it aside enough for me to slip past it. Once inside, I turned around. If I had to exit quickly again, this time I wanted it to be headfirst. Moss hovered at the entrance, his light beam playing over the area.

Without actually entering, he could see the section around the opening up to the log. He reached in as far as his arms allowed. I was aware that he was picking up and studying some debris on the floor, though I had messed up a lot of that as he pulled me out.

Satisfied that there were no other animals, I confirmed my first impression that I couldn't follow the spring back any farther. The floor was completely covered with junk. So far I hadn't touched the floor but was floating just a few inches above it. I saw rusty nails, lots of what looked like ashes dumped there from the stove, broken shards of crockery, and some deteriorated metal vessels like washtubs. No wonder the spring dried up—choked up was more like it.

With the opening blocked off, the water went underground, just as I had surmised.

Actually, I was disappointed. This second dive was an anticlimax. I don't know what I expected, but it was dull after the tussle with the turtle. All that debris had to be more than seventy or eighty years old, since Aunt Iris barely remembered the spring. And it really was junk of no use even as antiques.

Gramps and Granny didn't throw away anything until it was of no possible use. Most of the trash was probably rusted or rotted beyond repair before they disposed of it. Nothing interested me. My curiosity satisfied, I returned to the opening ready to swim out.

Moss blocked my way. He was holding something in his hand, studying it. When he saw me ready to emerge, he held up his left hand to ask me to stop. Then he showed me the object he was holding. It was a long, narrow animal bone about twelve inches long. He pointed to the cave floor at the opening to show where he found it. Then he pointed to the log. I understood his signals. He wanted me to look under it. In my struggle to get out before, I had bumped against the log. It was so deteriorated that the end nearest the opening had crumbled.

Even under water with his face encased in his mask, I could see Moss's excitement as he kept gesturing for me to look. He held up the bone and then made digging motions with his hand for me to investigate near the log.

It was interesting, I admitted, but I didn't feel the excitement of finding an animal bone that he seemed to feel. Could a wounded deer have crawled into here?

I doubted it. Too small an area. The bone was too large for muskrats, skunks, or other small mammals that might have died in the spring cave. More likely it was from a steer or hog that Gramps had butchered, dumping its carcass in here along with the other trash. On the farm, finding animal bones was pretty common.

Moss was crammed in the hole as far as he could go until his tank blocked his way. His actions communicated great excitement. I wasn't too particular now about disturbing the stuff on the floor as I'd seen all I wanted. I let myself down to the floor to do what Moss wanted. Kneeling, I laid my hand on the log to move it over. More pieces fell off until I found the hard core in the center that didn't crumble. Carefully holding it with both hands, I raised up the log and shoved it a couple of feet to the left, careful not to cloud the water with silt.

In the depression the log left on the cave floor, right beside my knees and facing me, was a stretched-out skeleton of a full-grown person.

Chapter Six

Once again in surprise and fright I dropped my light to the floor; its glow became buried in the bucket of ashes. The powerful beam from Moss's light wavered over the body for a moment, crossed my wet suit, and then spotted a portion of the ceiling above me as he reacted to the sight. The specter I saw on the floor was in too dim a light for me to see. Surely that grim figure was my overactive imagination brought on by my remembering a comment of my instructor the first time I entered an underwater cave in training: "One of my secret fears when I go diving is that I'll run across a body down here!"

Moss's light returned to the spot on the floor that I uncovered by moving the log. This was no imagination. Lying there prone was a complete skeleton, its skull turned so that it faced me and the left arm extending out toward me. All of the bones were in perfect order except those of the left arm and hand. Some of them were scattered toward the opening.

In horror I looked toward Moss, who was back-lighted in the opening. He was still holding the long bone. I realized then what must have happened. When he pulled me out of the cave in my confrontation with the turtle, I disturbed the arm, which was the only part of the body not covered by the log. My body or arms made contact with the skeleton's arm, messing up the bones and dragging close to the entrance the bone Moss found. He must have recognized it as human when he asked me to move the log.

We knew no signals to communicate our reactions in this circumstance. My first thought was what an extraordinary situation I was in. Though I was very much alive, I was inside a watery grave kneeling just inches from a dead body. A body dead long enough that all that remained was the skeleton. I forced myself to continue breathing regularly. I couldn't repeat my amateurish breathing behavior that I had exhibited on confronting the turtle. I took some slow, even breaths to steady myself.

My next thought was of all the trouble and unpleas-ant publicity this discovery might cause Moss—a dead body on his property. Maybe we could ignore it and pretend we hadn't seen it? No, I knew we couldn't do that. Anyway, I reasoned, he wouldn't be suspected of any wrongdoing. This person had been here for years. I knew that a body, with no remnants of clothing left, couldn't deteriorate to a skeleton in just the few months Moss had owned the land. That amount of decay would take many years. All of the old-fashioned relics around it proclaimed several decades had passed. Certainly more than the twenty years since my family had owned the place.

I gasped and again had to force myself to breathe regularly. This skeleton must come from my family's tenure on the land!

That horror was worse than discovering the body. I wanted out; I regretted my curiosity. Suddenly I hated Moss again. If he'd left the buildings alone and not built this lake, no one would ever have discovered the sinister secret hidden in the spring cave. But that was not fair. If I hadn't been so curious . . .

As I knelt there beside the body I heard a rapping. Under water it was difficult to tell where the sound came from. At first I imagined it coming from the skeleton. Facing me with its mutilated arm thrown out toward me, it seemed to be pleading for my help. Ridiculous! Then I looked up to see Moss banging on the rock entrance, trying to get my attention. He was frantically motioning with his arm for me to get out. That was exactly what I wanted. I nodded.

Scanning the area to memorize the scene, the position of the body, and the items near it—the bucket of ashes, the overturned skillet, and the little wagon wheel—I carefully rose from the floor so I wouldn't disturb anything else. This was now a crime scene, and I had seen enough police shows on television to know I shouldn't bother anything more than I'd already done.

As I slowly swam out of the cave, I noticed that the original course of the spring's route had carved out a path that curved around the body. Until the cave was recently flooded by the lake water, the body had rested on dry ground. On this exit I didn't scrape my tank on the opening or drag myself across the floor. I wasn't fleeing from a live and angry animal into whose temporary home I'd intruded, but from the quiet death grin of some long-gone human whose grave I had invaded.

By the time I got clear of the cave and hovered on a level with its entrance beside Moss, I was shaking perceptibly. At that moment, when Moss's worried brown eyes looked through my mask to my eyes, and he put his hand on my arm to comfort me, he was no longer a mere client whose place I was landscaping. Nor was he the enemy who had desecrated the Love-land buildings. Coming out of the dark tomb into the glistening sunlit water, I felt as if he and I were the only two people on earth. We were bound together by this nightmarish reality.

With his hand still on my arm, we ascended. The feel of his strong grip calmed me even though his hand trembled slightly. His touch was more comforting than the first time we surfaced after my confrontation with the turtle because this time we shared the experience equally. His touch pleased me on an emotional level not connected to my fear and the horror of our discovery.

Watching us from the boat, Connie was surprised that we returned so quickly. She supposed that, as I usually did, I would stay down as long as my air lasted. She hadn't seen any indications of what we found in the cave nor had our actions betrayed our fright.

"Well?" she asked when we didn't say anything. She looked first at Moss and then at me for an explanation. Dripping lake water, we both sat down in the rocking boat and automatically removed our masks, regulators, and tanks.

After the long look we shared just before we ascended, Moss and I hadn't glanced at each other. Our communication was through his touch on my arm. We sat dumbly, staring at the pools of water gathering in the boat from our wet suits and equipment.

"What's up, you guys?" Connie asked. Her head swung back and forth from me to Moss and back to me. "Did you see another prehistoric turtle or maybe a nest of snakes?" Her tone was lighthearted, but noticing our sober faces, she became worried.

We shook our heads. Moss glanced at me and then said to Connie, "No, nothing like that. More like ghosts." He didn't explain, but added, "I think I better call the sheriff. Paddle us to shore, Connie, please."

"What the . . . ?"

"We found a human skeleton in the cave." I had my trembling under control and could now say the words in a matter-of-fact tone, as if we had found some more rusty pots.

While Moss made the call from his pickup, I filled Connie in on what we found. I was still half thinking that I imagined it all; telling her helped me make the experience real. I was ready to think about what I should do.

"I've got to call Aunt Iris," I said.

"Why would you worry her about that?"

"Because I think the body came from the time my

family lived here. I've got to find out if she knows anything about it.''

"What a bummer! But, Darrah, even if she does know something, wouldn't it be better to leave her out of it? At least until you find out more about it.''

"You may be right. But she'll hear about it right away from my cousin Abby. When the sheriff gets here, it'll be in the police reports and the papers. I can't keep it from her. But you're right. I'll wait a bit, though I don't want her to hear it from someone else first.''

Racing through my mind were thoughts of what this might mean to my family, and that whatever trouble would ensue from finding the skeleton, it was all my fault for bringing it to light. Connie's main concern was whether it would affect our job with Moss. I assured her that the investigation, which would be confined to the lake, wouldn't slow us up. We could continue our work.

Moss returned with news that the sheriff would be right out. A diving team from a search-and-rescue unit from the city in a neighboring county would be here later in the afternoon. "I told the sheriff that he didn't need to hurry. The body was very old and had been there a long time. He didn't seem to believe me. He and the diving team are still coming right out.''

The pleasure in the outing and the thrill of diving again that the morning promised was ruined for me as I sat slumped over on one of the big rocks Carl and Allen had grouped near the lake's spillway just the day before. But both Moss and Connie were excited at the turn of events. Moss recovered quickly from his

shock. He and Connie were thrilled that we had uncovered a real mystery to solve. They put out several
theories to explain the dead body in the cave.

Always the romantic, Connie thought it was a girl
who had crawled into the cave to die when her lover
left her. Standing near me and clenching her hands in
her enthusiasm, she invented a complete scenario of
what might have happened to the left-at-the-altar girl.

I didn't dare verbalize what I feared—that it was a
murder from Gramps's time.

"From what I saw, it must be ancient," Moss said.
"I think it's from the Bluff Dweller era. They buried
their dead in caves. And when I built the lake and
flooded the cave, everything inside got moved
around." His eyes were full of wonder. "I think that's
the most likely explanation, don't you, Darrah?" I
liked the way he said my name, slowly, as if savoring
the sound as he rolled the double Rs over his tongue.

I had to admit it sounded reasonable. *Please let that
be the explanation instead of what I'm thinking!* I
pleaded silently. Seeing all of Gramps's stuff in there
naturally pointed to him and the dead person being
connected in some way to our family. But my fears
weren't as logical as the Bluff Dweller theory. I reasoned it out. Being a big man, both tall and stout,
Gramps couldn't have crawled into the cave himself
to put the body inside. The position of the body
showed that it was obviously dragged inside. But what
about all of his trash that I saw in the cave? Ah! That
stuff was all near the opening. The floor of the rest of
the chamber behind the log was bare. So probably
what happened was this: not having any idea that there

was a body in there, Gramps just stuffed the trash in at the entrance to keep children from hurting themselves, just as he said.

"Yes, that must be right," I answered Moss. "The Bluff Dwellers were a lot smaller than we are. They could easily have entered and buried someone in there." Then I remembered the oak log on top of the body. That certainly wasn't decayed enough to come from that ancient time. Perhaps, though, the log being exactly on top of the body could be just a coincidence; it was probably thrown inside like the other items. Even as I explained away the log, something about the size of the skeleton wasn't quite right.

"Maybe there is more than one body in there," Moss said.

"Could be," I said. Though I wanted the Indian theory to be the correct one, I found more reasons against it. "The Ozark Bluff Dwellers buried their dead in grass-lined graves with stones on top to protect them from animals. This body wasn't buried that way. It was vulnerable."

"It is now," Moss said, "but how long ago would that have been? A thousand years?" When I nodded, he continued, "During that time the spring probably changed many times, just like it did when I dug down to it. Maybe it didn't even flow out of that cave when the body was buried there. Then years of heavy rains caused it to start. The spring gushing forth could have washed away the dirt and rocks."

The more he talked the more reasonable it sounded. I was feeling much better. Moss was right. The mystery was from hundreds of years ago. But, nevertheless, I was going to stick around until the sheriff and the search-and-rescue team arrived.

Always prepared for any contingency, Connie had anticipated that we might want some lunch. She pulled out a loaded ice cooler from behind the pickup seat. Feeling like three kids acting out an imaginary adventure, we found a shady spot under some black walnut trees to spread out Connie's snacks. Without even discussing where we would eat, we automatically left the bare lake area for the undisturbed woods. I admitted, though, that the loads of rich topsoil our workers had spread over the bank greatly softened the raw look. We had already smoothed out and seeded most of the bank and part of the area around the lake. Fresh straw was neatly spread out to protect the seeds. In just days there would be a green cast over it.

We found a perfect spot up the hill, on the thick bluegrass carpet under the bright yellow leaves of the largest walnut tree. Pushing aside the green walnuts that had fallen, Connie spread out the blanket she always carried in the truck for emergencies. Laughing at her foresight, we sat in a circle around the cooler. She passed out sandwiches, chips, pickles, and cold sodas.

We couldn't stop talking about the skeleton. "Isn't it great?" Moss said to me. "I hired you to return the land to an earlier time, and first I find that your family lived here for several generations, and now we find evidence of people who lived here ages ago."

"It's so romantic," Connie said. She was still sure the body was of a spurned lover, but now she placed it back in the Stone Age when such betrayals meant dishonor and suicide.

Connie's comment aside, I had to admit that it was an intriguing coincidence. Here was Moss with his love of the land. And me with my love of the land and my family. And now we discovered a much older person who probably loved the land and had a family. But my persistent worry returned. Since the eras of the Bluff Dwellers and later the Osages, the only people living on the land were Lovelands. They were the ones who exploited the land. Did they also exploit people? I couldn't shake the thought that they had something to do with that body. I almost lost my good mood until I remembered Aunt Iris telling me that I had an opportunity to turn the farm around, and when I finished, it would be better than it had ever been.

Moss had the best theory. A burial site of one of the earliest inhabitants on the land would add to the aura of the place. I wondered if I could in some way incorporate that feeling into my landscaping designs.

The noise of vehicles on the drive alerted us that we had company. Two white cars from the sheriff's department crept down the hill, followed by an official-looking black van.

"Looks like the search-and-rescue team is here, too." Connie said.

We gathered up our lunch and hurried to the lake just as the officers pulled up to the lake's spillway. Two men from the van were suiting up for the dive. Everyone gathered around Moss and me as we told them what we discovered. Moss began his account about the opening up of the spring with the bulldozer and then told of my curiosity about the spring cave and taking advantage of the spring to practice diving. He described both dives, the turtle encounter that revealed the body's arm, and then actually finding the skeleton.

I said nothing about any earlier history. The sheriff didn't even know that I had any connection with the place. I hoped that my family would not be a factor. Besides, I had convinced myself that the body was prehistoric.

Moss and I took the two divers in the boat out into the lake and pointed out the spring. They were armed with bags, cameras, powerful lights, and other forensic equipment they might need.

Although we wanted to dive with them, the sheriff vetoed it. "Too many down there. Let the team do its work."

Our instructions were to return to shore after the men dived to let the sheriff take the boat out to see the site and watch the activity.

For the next couple of hours, the three of us had to cool our heels, waiting for any information. Since we could see the activity at the spring better from the bank, we stationed ourselves there, even though I was worried about us messing up our new seeding. Connie spread out her blanket again and we sat down to wait.

The team dived several times. The first dive took the longest. One man entered the cave, while the other watched from the entrance just as Moss and I had done. I knew the inside man was photographing the area. After that he brought out bags of items which they brought up to the boat—the bones and probably some of the junk around the body. Finally, about four o'clock, they finished and paddled ashore.

Ignoring me, which was logical because this was Moss's place, the sheriff and team gave their first assessment.

"My first evaluation will have to be verified by lab tests, but this is what I think," the team leader said. "The body is a male about five feet, eight inches tall. He is rather small boned, and was thin. I'd judge he was about forty years old. Cause of death seems to be from a bullet embedded in his spine just behind his heart. Looks like from a Colt pistol. It appears that the body, already dead or dying, was dragged on its stomach, headfirst, into the spring cave and dumped on dry ground beside the spring branch. Another interesting fact: the right hand of the man, which was under his body, was broken."

Turning to me he continued, "The log that you said you moved off of the body was probably put there at the same time to hide the body. Maybe even some of the items around it were put there then, too, but that is difficult to say. The lake water flooding the cave could have washed them near the body." He turned to Moss. "You said that the spring was dry and the cave opening covered when you dug the lake?"

"Yes," Moss said. "There was no evidence of any water. There was a ditch running down here, but that's all."

My stomach turned over. My clasped hands were clammy. I held my breath. "How long ago do you estimate this happened?" I asked, my voice higher than usual.

The two divers looked at each other, estimating. The second said, "Seventy-five to eighty years, maybe?"

The first diver nodded. "Eighty is about right. We'll know for sure after some tests."

There went the Bluff Dweller theory, putting it right smack in Gramps's time. Even during Aunt Iris's childhood!

Everyone was so intent on listening to the divers' talk that no one noticed me. I bent over, almost sick to my stomach. I felt dizzy. Then I straightened up and forced myself to act normal. No way was I going to divulge what I was thinking.

"Well," the sheriff said, relief showing on his face. "If the murder was that long ago, then we don't need to have a full-scale investigation. I'll check for any missing persons about that time. But I've lived in this end of the county all my life. I've never heard of any nor seen any record of any."

When the sheriff's cars and the van left, Connie, Moss, and I stood side by side on the lakeshore watching them drive cautiously up the steep, narrow drive.

"Well!" Connie was the first to say anything. She couldn't tolerate any silences. "Now it's a murder mystery."

Moss was watching me. Even if Connie hadn't put all the facts together, I could tell by his supportive look that he had figured out that the time of the murder put it during my great-grandfather's time, the family member I had mentioned to him several times. The problem, if there was one, was not Moss's, but it might be mine.

"Darrah," he said softly, "what are you thinking?"

"I'm thinking that I've got to go see Aunt Iris." I didn't explain who she was though he seemed to know.

Moss nodded. "May I go with you?"

"I'd like that," I said. From the moment that morning when we discovered the body and I feared what it might mean, I knew that I needed Moss with me to find out the truth.

Connie sent me a surprised look at my changed attitude toward Moss. I hadn't ever taken her to visit my aunt.

"Shall we go now?" Moss asked.

"Yes."

Chapter Seven

Aunt Iris listened carefully while I told her about
our dive. She laughed at the episode with the turtle.
But when I started to tell of the second dive, her eyebrows contracted and her fists clenched. Her eyes
flickered from me to Moss, who hadn't said anything
after greeting her.

"What's the matter, Aunt Iris?" I stopped my story
to ask. She was taking short breaths.

"I remembered something. It's nothing. Just an old
nightmare." She patted my knee. "Go on, child. I
know you didn't come to tell me about facing down
a snapping turtle and finding all that rubbish in there.
There's something more, isn't there?"

"Yes," I said softly.

Moss's expression encouraged me to continue. Aunt
Iris didn't miss his signal. She watched me carefully.

"In our second dive, I moved the log and ex-

89

posed . . .'' I didn't know how else to tell her but straight out.

"Exposed what?"

"A complete skeleton."

Her eyes showed more shock than I'd expected, more like fear. She gave a gasp. Her hand clenched my leg in a viselike grip. Before I lost my nerve, I blurted out the search-and-rescue team's preliminary findings, that it was the skeleton of a man who had been shot seventy-five to eighty years ago.

"Do you know something, Miss Loveland?" Moss asked, his voice gentle, his eyes concerned.

"I don't know!" Her voice was very weak; she had trouble speaking. She cleared her throat to make her voice louder. "Over the years I have convinced myself that it was only a nightmare that I used to have when I was a little girl. I reasoned that since I had it so often, I began to think it was real. Until the other night, I hadn't had the dream for a long time. I had it again the night after you drove me down to the home place. But I never did convince myself entirely that it was only a dream." Her voice became raspy.

I brought her a drink of water. She sipped a little, her hand trembling slightly. "With what you just said that you found, I know now that it wasn't just a nightmare. It happened. And I am the only one who knows. Poor Papa!" She paused a couple of seconds, rocking her body back and forth in her chair. Then, putting thoughts of others before herself as she had done all her life, she asked Moss, "Will you be in any trouble with a body found on your land?"

"No," he said softly, leaning toward her to touch

her veined hand. "When the sheriff learned that the body was that old, he didn't seem too interested. I don't think he'll pursue it except to search for reports of any missing persons from around here about that time."

"He won't find any."

"Then that will be the end of it," he said.

"How do you know he won't find any missing persons, Aunt Iris?"

"I can't tell you."

"You would have been very small at the time, about . . ."

"I was eight." She didn't hesitate to figure up her age, but blurted it out.

"What happened?" I urged her quietly.

"I've never told a soul. I can't tell you."

"If you know something, you must tell. What happened?" I urged.

She looked at me in anguish. Sipping some more water as if that would give her the strength to tell, she said, "I never really knew what happened, and it was so long ago. I've tried very hard to forget it, to convince myself that it didn't happen." Her hand holding the glass trembled. I took the glass and set it on the stand beside her chair. Moss still held her other hand.

She studied Moss's face, which was filled with compassion. Apparently she was satisfied with what she saw, for she continued with a bit more spirit. "I like you, Moss. Even when you almost ran over us with your truck, I liked the looks of you. You look even better now. With quick thinking and reflexes, you saved us then. Darrah and I are probably in a more vulnerable position now than we were that day. I have a feeling you can help us avoid another collision.''

Moss simply said, ''I'll do what I can.''

Aunt Iris gave a feeble smile. ''I'm glad that you are the one who owns the home place.'' She didn't mention the missing buildings. Compared to a murder, I guess she reasoned that the razed house and barn didn't seem important. ''And now since the body was found on your land and since it must have some connection back to Darrah's kin, I guess I should tell you both. But don't either of you tell a single soul.''

We both promised. ''After all, what happened almost eighty years ago shouldn't affect any of us now,'' I said. Even as I said it, I knew it wasn't true. So did Moss and Aunt Iris. Just finding the skeleton was already changing us. What would discovering the murderer do to us?

Aunt Iris sipped some more water. ''The sheriff won't find any reports of missing persons because the man wasn't from this part of the country. No one around here knew him, so they wouldn't know he was missing.'' She paused. Waiting for her continue, neither Moss nor I said anything. ''It was in the fall of 1920, I remember because I just had my eighth birthday and Papa gave me one of those miniature glass suitcases filled with candy. I'd never had anything so fine. It happened in the late afternoon. Papa, my baby brother, and I were the only ones at the house. Mama and my brother, Arnie, had gone up to the bluff pasture after the cows. Papa was out in the front, getting a bucket of water, I think, while I was minding the baby as I often did.

"But I better start earlier than that to give Moss the background." Aunt Iris was calm now. She sipped occasionally on the water, and as she got into her story, her voice strengthened.

The Lovelands were among the very first Americans to settle in the area after the Louisiana Purchase of 1803. In 1820, three brothers and their families moved from Tennessee and bought land along the river at $1.25 an acre. The land passed down in the family until Aunt Iris's father, Cyrus Loveland, inherited 160 acres as a young man. He had no money to build a decent house for his family. The old, original log home down by the fields that sometimes was affected by high water was the only building. He wanted more for his family—his wife Mabel and the two small children, Iris and Arnie. So he went west to Colorado to the gold fields in hopes of getting a stake. He returned several months later with enough money to build their house and big barn. Both buildings were the finest in the neighborhood at that time.

The family grew and prospered because of their prodigious work effort, Cyrus's skill and knowledge of the land, and Mabel's love and care.

Then not long after they had moved into the new house, Iris, alone in the house minding the new baby, heard the dog bark. She looked outside and noticed a man riding up to the gate on horseback. He leaned down from the saddle, opened the gate, and closed it behind him. His being able to do that without dismounting impressed Iris. The only other person she knew with a horse trained well enough to do that was her father.

Cyrus was at the pump getting a bucket of water. He dropped his bucket and hurried down the driveway toward the visitor. He met him by the draw, or ditch, that crossed the drive. The stranger dismounted and, gesturing angrily with his arms, advanced upon Cyrus. He limped a little bit. Cyrus stood his ground. The two men argued. Iris was too far away to hear their words but from their gestures and body language, she recognized a bitter confrontation. Since her father sometimes lost his temper, she wasn't too worried about the disagreement outside. He could take care of himself.

When the baby cried, she attended to him and didn't see what happened next. She heard some more loud voices and then she heard a gunshot. Since men hunted in the woods and on the river, hearing a gun was not unusual. However, this sound was very close to the house; it came from the driveway where the men were. Frightened, she grabbed the baby and ran upstairs to her new room, covering both of them with a quilt. She was sure that the man had killed her father and would be after her next.

Nothing happened. No more gunshots, loud shouts, or footsteps. No doors opened. Later, after her mother and Arnie returned with the cows, Cyrus strolled into the house from the barn just as usual. He showed no signs of any struggle, either physical or emotional. There was even a fresh bucket of water on the wash-stand. The family did the milking and tended to the chickens. Everything was normal. In no way did Cyrus indicate any problem nor did he mention the visitor.

Iris's relief that her father was not killed changed to the fear that he killed the stranger. Afraid that if she verbalized it, it would be true, she said nothing to either parent. While they were busy, she ran out to the driveway. There was no stranger or any evidence to show what she witnessed and heard. With great relief, she reasoned that the man got back on his horse and left; the shot she heard was merely a neighbor hunting.

"But you now think that the skeleton we found in the spring was the stranger?" I asked when Aunt Iris dropped her hands in her lap, indicating that she was finished.

She nodded. "I knew something bad happened. I just knew. Why else would I be haunted by it all these years?"

"What did the stranger look like?" Moss asked.

"Well, he was older than my father. Not as tall and very thin. While they were arguing I thought that the man was foolish to think he could win over my father, who was bigger and stronger. Oh yes, I remember that he wore a big western hat and jeans—what we used to call overall pants. I noticed them because the men in the Ozarks didn't wear clothes like that. They wore bib overalls and ordinary straw or felt hats. This man was different. Anyone would notice him."

Moss and I glanced at each other before I replied. "That description fits what the diver said about the body in the cave. Except for the clothing, of course. They had all rotted away."

None of us said anything for a couple of minutes. Aunt Iris played with her hands and wiped her face with her handkerchief. Then she asked, "Do you think that my father could have shot that man and dragged him into the spring cave to hide him?"

"No! Not possible." Even though that was just what I had been thinking, I hadn't said it out loud.

"What else could it be?" she asked.

We couldn't answer that.

"Did your father carry a gun with him around the place?" Moss asked.

"No, of course not."

"Then he wouldn't have had a gun to shoot the man?"

"No, I'm sure of that."

"Did he own a Colt?" I asked.

"No, just shotguns. Twelve gauge and a four-ten. No pistols." She shook her head as if that cleared him. Then she frowned again. "Oh-h-h! He did have a Colt pistol. He never used it, but when Arnie graduated from high school, Papa gave it to him. I'd forgotten that."

The black mood settled on us again.

"Supposing Cyrus killed the stranger, then what happened to the horse he was riding?" Moss asked.

"Yeah." I brightened. A loose horse in the neighborhood would have posed problems.

"Papa was always trading horses. He probably made more money trading than farming, if the truth were told. None of us would have thought anything about a new horse in the barn."

"Was there a new horse about that time?" I asked.

"Goodness, child, I don't remember. He had so many. I used to ride his horses." She thought for a moment. "There was one gelding that he called Goldie that he wouldn't let me ride. I don't remember if that was at that time or not. He kept it for several months. It was skittish. Come to think of it, Papa never rode him either—something about his mouth, I think."

"What happened to him?"

"Traded him off to a guy from Arkansas who came through looking for horses. I remember that because he traded him for a pony that he gave to me."

"Why did he call the horse Goldie?" I asked. "That's more a name for a mare, not a gelding. Was he a palomino?"

"No, a bay."

"And the color of the stranger's horse," Moss asked, "did you notice that?"

"Of course. Just like you would remember the color of a strange car that drove in. Then most people rode horses. Not too many people had cars in the hills at that time. Sure I noticed the horse. I couldn't see people's faces from that distance, but I could sure see the horse."

"Well, what color was the horse?"

"Everything points to my father!" She was rubbing her hands and grabbing one wrist with the other hand. The raised blue veins and the numerous brown spots made her almost-transparent skin seem even more colorless. "The horse the stranger was riding was a bay," she finally said.

She put her hands over her face. When she removed

them, her determined eyes looked hard at each of us. "You promised you wouldn't tell anyone."

"No way," I said, sneaking a look at Moss to see his reaction. It wasn't his family's reputation at stake.

"Everything you've said is all circumstantial and probably coincidental," he said, "as well as unreliable memories and the frightened imagination of a child. Yes, I promise not to tell."

Aunt Iris patted my leg and gave me her I-knew-I-was-right-about-him grin.

Moss didn't miss her reaction. He smiled at her. "You can count on me. We're all in this together. But there must be something Darrah and I can do to find out for sure what happened. We'll investigate some and then we'll let you be the one to divulge the information if you think it necessary."

"What can you do? I'm the only living person who knows anything. Even Papa never knew what I saw and heard. No one ever came asking about the stranger, and as far as I know no one else even saw him ride into the neighborhood. At least no one ever mentioned it."

"I can make some queries in Colorado," Moss said. "The man might have been from the mines where Cyrus worked. His western clothes indicated that."

"And Gramps calling his horse Goldie," I said. "Maybe from the gold mines? Do you know where he went or what mines?" Colorado gold mines seemed too vague a place to start.

Aunt Iris started to shake her head, but then her eyes brightened. "Darrah girl, bring me my shoe box of old letters. That one there on the back shelf of the closet.'' When I handed the box to her, she pawed through the letters quickly until she found a faded envelope. ''Here it is. Papa sent this to me while he was gone. The first letter I ever got. I was hardly old enough to read it myself.'' She handed it to me. The cancellation stamp on the outside was faded and unreadable. Part of the letter was also illegible.

''May I take this envelope with me?'' Moss asked. ''I know someone who can bring out the lettering. We might be able to read the stamp.''

''Sure. I think he was somewhere near Colorado Springs, if that helps any,'' she said. ''He used to talk about Pikes Peak.''

''Yeah,'' I said, brightening with bits from my own memory. ''One of my favorite stories he used to tell was when he climbed Pikes Peak in a snowstorm.'' I studied the postmark on the envelope. ''Looks like the town begins with a G.''

Aunt Iris got out her atlas and pointed to a spot in the middle of the map of Colorado. ''Here, Darrah girl, look at this fine print with your young eyes. Isn't that Goldfield?''

I was excited. ''Goldfield! Gramps used to say that, but I thought it was just a generic term for the gold mines.''

''That narrows it down considerably,'' Moss said. His eyes were dancing with the challenge of solving a real mystery on his place. I was surprised at myself for thinking of the farm as ''his place.''

''I'll get right on this,'' he said. ''I can search with my computer. You'd be surprised what I can find out.

I'll look for missing persons from that area and try to find just where Cyrus Loveland staked his claim.''

"And after we get the official results back from the sheriff," I said, "I'm going to dive back into that cave and search again. I may find something the team may have missed. There has to be something left, a button, pocketknife, or something.''

"And if we discover that my father did kill the man?" Aunt Iris asked.

"Then we'll know for sure," I said. "But I can't believe it. Gramps, in spite of being such a big man, was a gentle one. One Easter I remember him getting upset because one of us kids trampled his daffodils.''

"And many times," Aunt Iris said, "I saw him cup a baby chick in his hands to warm it up when it got lost from its mother.''

"Doesn't sound like a man who would murder someone and then conceal him in a cave," Moss said.

"Absolutely not," Aunt Iris said. "But he did have a bad temper.''

"But he never hurt anything," I said.

"No, he didn't even whip balking cows or bucking horses. He talked them into doing what he wanted.''

"Then let's be optimistic and assume that we will find out he wasn't involved," Moss said. "There could be other facts we know nothing about.''

We sat for a few minutes digesting everything we learned and talked about. I felt better, and I'm sure that Aunt Iris did, too. With the purpose of our visit completed, I became aware of wonderful aromas coming from her little kitchen. She got out of her chair, and without her walker but putting her hand on each piece of furniture as she went to steady herself, opened the oven door. Inside was a blackberry cobbler, the purple juice bubbling up around the edges.

"I thought you might be hungry," she said with a wink at Moss. "So after Darrah called to say you were coming, I stirred up this cobbler. Do you like it with ice cream?"

By the time we left, Moss and my aunt were best buddies. He completely won her over. To be frank, he was succeeding pretty well with me, also. Holding on to his arm, she accompanied us to the door. Moss squeezed her hand and gave her a kiss on her cheek. "Thanks for the pie," he said. Realizing that she and I might have something to say privately, he walked out to his pickup.

"I'm really sorry about all this, Aunt Iris. I had no idea what I would find when I made that dive."

"Don't fret on it, Darrah girl. It's probably a good thing. I don't think I'll have the nightmare again. It's time to put it to rest once and for all."

"What if we find that Gramps . . ."

"Don't even think of that. You won't." She waved to Moss, who was at the opened passenger door waiting for me. Then she cocked her head toward him and said, "He's a keeper."

Chapter Eight

I was obsessed with thinking about the body in the cave. Connie had to keep me focused on our job while we waited for both the official results from the sheriff's investigation and from Moss's probing into the 1920 records at Goldfield, Colorado. He hadn't been able to read anything more from Gramps's letter to Aunt Iris. Working around the lake aggravated my anxiety. I couldn't keep my mind on plants and designs; all I could think of was Gramps. And Moss. The two men merged in my mind.

I wanted to dive again right away to see if I could find some clue that the diving team had missed, but Moss made me promise to wait for him. Connie was strongly against me diving another time. No way would she accompany me, so I was forced to wait for Moss to be my partner. I carried my scuba equipment with me to be ready when he came to the farm. I figured that he would also have his equipment with him, for he seemed as eager as I to dive again.

The lake was filling steadily. We wanted to shape the contours and curves of the spillway branch before the spring filled the lake and began to run over. Connie surveyed the area to mark the natural path the water would follow. I added to the aesthetics of the flow with strategically placed boulders our workers hauled up from the river. When Moss finally arrived, I was arranging some weathered and moss-covered stones to create a small waterfall just upstream from the bridge our crew was constructing.

"I just heard from the sheriff," he said as I dropped my crowbar and ran to him. He looked great in tan, freshly pressed jeans and a brown shirt that matched his hair. With easy grace, he stepped out of his pickup, his expression telling me he was glad to see me. I was equally happy to see him, too, but not only for the news he might have or to see his reaction to what we had done since his last visit. I just felt more alive when he was with me. Safer, too, somehow, as if his presence would protect me from the ghost from the cave.

He glanced around quickly in enthusiastic approval of our progress. He started to comment about it, but he could tell from my eager face that I was more anxious to hear what the sheriff learned than his reaction to our work. "The diver's first evaluation was correct," he said. "The bones belong to a man, a Caucasian, about forty years old. He was killed somewhere else by a Colt pistol shot to the heart. The bullet pierced it and lodged in his spine. He was then dragged headfirst into the cave and dumped on his stomach where we found him.''

I held my breath. ''When did this happen?''

''Eighty years ago.''

I stiffened as my heart took a nosedive. Somehow, I'd convinced myself that the divers' first estimate about the date was wrong.

Moss's eyes never left my face as he continued, ''The sheriff said there were no local records of unsolved missing persons around that time. He has filed the information away and closed the case, since nobody has come forward. Anyone still living would have been a small child at the time. So unless someone shows any interest, and I told him I didn't want any investigation, he will have the body buried. Case closed.'' He grinned and touched my arm. ''Now we're free to do our own detective work, Darrah.'' I loved the way he rolled the double Rs in my name.

''Did you say anything to him about what Aunt Iris . . .''

''No, of course not. Even if I hadn't promised her, I wouldn't have. No use stirring up something long buried. Besides, we really don't know anything for sure.''

''What about publicity?'' I had looked for big headlines in the local paper about a murder. All I found was a short account on the back page that gave very few details. It was more a query, asking for information anyone might have.

Moss grinned. ''I know the editor and convinced him to downplay it. One of his reporters wanted to make a big spread on the front page about the murder, but the editor bumped it to the back with just the official short notice. Actually he wasn't too interested. It's more history than news, and as you know, he isn't much into local history.''

''Yes, I know.'' He was a city journalist who bought the *Timberton Daily Times*. He resisted printing the historical and nostalgic articles many local people enjoyed.

Moss grinned. ''There's another consideration. He undoubtedly thought about all the advertising Moss Industries gives his paper. He was perfectly willing to do as I asked.''

''You didn't bribe him, did you?''

''No, didn't have to. He's a good businessman. It didn't hurt that his son works for us, too.''

I was greatly relieved that I didn't have to worry about the damage the publicity would have done to our family's reputation. Any skeletons in the closet would stay with us and Aunt Iris. I groaned at the reality of that figure of speech.

''Have you found out anything from Colorado?''

''Not yet. I'm working on it.'' Now that he had shared his news, he looked more closely at the progress we'd made. ''You really work fast. It's looking even better than I envisioned it from your plans.''

''When I drew them, I didn't know how strong the spring was. It will put out enough flow to make a small but steady brooklet. I've added some extra rocks and plants to take advantage of a year-round, running stream of water.''

''Like that waterfall?'' He had just noticed it. His

eyebrows lifted in pleasure. "It's incredible!" He hugged me in his delight.

"We put it here close to the driveway to make an intriguing entrance." I managed to speak in my business tone, even though the feel of his arms still warmed me. "Behind it we'll plant some bamboo and native cane to camouflage the lake bank. As you cross the bridge, the view of the waterfall and the curving spring branch leads you up the drive around the embankment to get the surprise effect of the entire lake scene. Do you like it?"

"Absolutely! You truly are magic."

"That's us."

I put my finger to my lips and pointed to a little chipmunk that darted from between the rocks and jumped up the bank out of sight in some leaves. Moss grinned happily, grabbed my hand, and pulled me with him as he walked around the area inspecting our progress. When he had inspected every last detail, he let go of my hand, looked at me, removed my floppy hat, and grinned. "Ready to dive again?"

Even though I was happy to talk about the job, I had to force myself to keep focused on it. My two men kept pushing themselves foremost in my mind— the one close to me now whose touch and searching eyes were causing me so much turmoil, and Gramps, my childhood idol, who was connected in some way to the murdered man. Conducting my business was automatic with me. Clients being pleased or disappointed I could handle with aplomb. But Moss's nearness and obvious interest in me, coupled with

Gramps's involvement in a murder? I didn't know how much longer I could keep my cool demeanor.

"Ready and anxious," I said. "I brought my gear. Did you?"

He nodded and pointed back to his vehicle. "Let's get suited up."

We didn't bother using the boat this time. We weren't concerned with stirring up the bottom, as we had learned on our previous dives that the murky lake water didn't affect the spring. Its steady output quickly cleared the water near the cave. Holding hands, we waded into the lake from the point in the embankment nearest to the cave. After just a few steps, the lake bottom soon fell away beneath our feet and water covered our hooded heads. When we sank to the level of the rock ledge and the mouth of the cave, Moss let go of my hand and signaled for me to lead.

Remembering the snapping turtle, I paused to shine my light inside. Though I couldn't see anything, an animal could be lurking behind any of the piles of litter on the floor. I rapped on the rocks with my knife, knowing that the sound would carry well underwater and hopefully scare out any animal.

Moss signaled for me to enter. With all the construction work going on, there had been too much commotion for any animal to stick around. I just wanted to make sure. I agreed. It was safe.

Just as we had done a few days before, I eased myself carefully into the cave while he hovered at the entrance. We had agreed that he would reach into the cave as far as he could to sift through everything on the floor. I would comb the interior. We both knew we'd feel better if we gave it another go.

If I hadn't known the diving team had been in the cave, I wouldn't have suspected it. The flow of the spring had erased any evidence. The log, still resting in its new position where I pushed it, already looked natural there. Small debris and a thin layer of silt had settled over the spot where the log covered the body. Many of the bigger items, washtubs and pots, were still where I remembered seeing them. It looked like the divers removed only the body and searched only the area immediately around it.

Moss and I had reasoned that anything we could find to help identify the body would be either right where the body lay or on the cave floor in a straight path from the opening where the body had been dragged in. Moss's part was to search the path. His long arm reached almost to where the skeleton's feet had rested. Using his fingers like a comb, he would sift through the few inches of silt down to the solid rock bed. I was to start where I remembered the skull lay and work back toward Moss.

Our search was a long shot. I knew the trained search-and-rescue team had been thorough, but I needed to do my own probe, more to ease my mind about Gramps. And, I admitted, it was an excuse to dive again with Moss. Being entombed with him in this underwater cell was exotic, more romantic than anything I'd ever experienced. Though we were both encased in wet suits, hoods, and masks, and dependent on our tanks for every breath, we were more together than in an embrace. We were alone in an aquatic fairyland, suspended in space and time. The real world temporarily ceased to exist.

My search was hampered by the currents flowing between us. With an effort, I took my eyes from him to guide my hands in fingering through the silt on the floor.

Even as I was sifting through the fine sand, the ashes, and rotted vegetative materials that were clearly lit by my light, I was sure that our efforts were futile. Where the skull lay, the cave floor was solid rock. As I moved back toward the opening, I found patches of clay. I stuck my fingers into the soft clay to dig out a handful and formed it into a ball. Feeling playful, I tried to throw it at Moss. Underwater dodgeball didn't work. The clay ball floated to the floor a couple of feet short of Moss's laughing face.

In my search when I reached the spot where the body's midsection rested, I forced my fingers through the gummy clay. I hoped to find buttons, a belt buckle, suspender clasp, or anything durable remaining from his clothing. Aunt Iris said he wore jeans. He would have worn a belt. And lying on his stomach, any metals from his clothing would have fallen to the clay floor when the clothing rotted away. I found several small rocks and lots of smooth pebbles. I filled my bag with them, planning to put them along the spring branch.

My fingers scraped against a flat, round rock different from anything I'd found. It was about three inches in circumference. I wiped off the clay and scraped away the harder corrosion. It was a belt buckle—a big silver buckle that men in the West wear! I held it up for Moss to see. He motioned for me to bring it to him. With bubbles escaping us and bouncing on the ceiling, I watched as he scraped off more crusty coating with his knife. Even under water in the half-natural and half-artificial light of the cave opening, we could clearly see a large C raised above an ornate background design.

Through his mask, I read the excitement in Moss's eyes as he undoubtedly did in mine. Moss clenched his fist and shook it. I motioned that I would search some more. He signaled okay. Our success in finding the buckle elated us.

We found nothing else though we stayed as long as our air supply let us. We surfaced, removed our masks, and climbed out on the pond bank where we entered. We stood close together studying the buckle.

"I can narrow my search for someone whose last name begins with a C," Moss said, the excitement of discovery in his voice.

That was my first thought, too. Then my thrill of discovery turned to dread. "Maybe the C stands for a first name?" I was thinking of Gramps. His first name was Cyrus. Could this be his buckle? No, he wouldn't have owned one as ornate as this. He always wore overalls. On the few times he dressed up in a suit, like for funerals, he wore suspenders and a vest. No, this buckle didn't point to Gramps. It had to be the stranger's. Aunt Iris described him wearing western garb. It all fit. We were unraveling the mystery piece by piece.

Moss shook his head. "No, it's for a last name. A man wouldn't use his first initial."

We removed our diving gear and stored it in our

trucks. While we were discussing what the buckle could mean, Moss polished it. It was a beautiful piece of silver, well crafted. Eighty years ago it must have cost quite a bit. Definitely not Gramps's. He never spent money on fancy clothing.

Elbow Jurgen pulled up, his johnboat in the back of his old Chevy pickup. He waved at us from his truck window as we walked toward him. He was on his way to the river to fish the Loveland Eddy. Moss had told me that he greatly enjoyed Elbow's company and they had become fishing buddies. Moss invited him to put into the river from his place anytime he wanted, so he wouldn't have to float down to the eddy from the low-water bridge and paddle back.

"That there's a fine buckle," Elbow said, noticing it in Moss's hands.

"Yeah, it is." Moss cupped the buckle with his other hand and tried to change the subject. "Good day for bass to be biting."

Elbow ignored his fishing comment and reached for the buckle. "Can I see it?" Reluctantly Moss handed it to him. Elbow studied it for a few seconds, the lines drawing around his toothless mouth. "Don't see many like that."

"No, it is unusual."

"I saw one like it when I was a boy."

I quickly did some figuring in my head. Elbow was a couple of years older than Aunt Iris. He had lived on the same farm all his life—the farm we passed on the main road before turning off onto the lane leading to the river-bottom farms. Could he have seen something when he was a boy?

Moss was downplaying the buckle and trying to get the old man's attention from it. Even though I knew he didn't want to talk about it to Elbow, I asked, "When was that, Elbow? When did you see one like it?"

Sometimes it was dangerous to ask Elbow such a leading question, that is, unless you had lots of time to listen to his long-winded answer that usually ended up with a moral. I was playing on a hunch that we might discover something, since he was the only neighbor still living who might have been near the farm that day in the fall of 1920.

"I saw one like that on a feller back when I was a boy—'long about ten or twelve years old, I was." He ran his gnarled forefinger over the buckle's surface. "It even had a big C on it just like this one."

Moss glanced quickly at me. He understood why I questioned Elbow. "Tell us about it," he said.

"Well, I recollect 'cause this feller looked just like the cowboys in them dime novels I read. He didn't look like nobody 'round here."

"What did he look like?"

"Well, he had on one of them big ten-gallon hats. Black with some silver braiding on it."

"How big was he?"

"He looked big to me, but I was a scrawny kid. Hard to tell, 'cause he was sitting up there on that big bay horse that was prancing around. Average-size man, I'd judge. Five-eight or -nine."

"Did he wear a gun like the cowboys in the movies?" I asked.

"Sure did. In a holster strapped around his waist. It

was under his long coat that was parted, like to hang down on either side of the saddle. I saw it.''

Elbow's faded blue eyes flickered from me to Moss. He noticed our agitation and, spurred on by our interest, continued, ''Yeah, stopped by our house and asked directions to Cyrus's place.''

''He did!'' I forced myself to control my emotions so the keen old man wouldn't be too suspicious.

''Yep. Never seen him again, though. I later asked Cyrus about him, but Cyrus just said he was someone he knew from out West a-comin' to trade horses.'' Elbow chuckled. ''Then Cyrus told me a long story about horse swapping, kind of like he didn't want me to ask any more questions about the stranger. He looked kind of sadlike. But that Cyrus, he was a caution. He used to tell me some whoppers. Real big windies, you betcha.''

Elbow paused a second. ''Well, I've bothered you folks enough. I see you're busy. I'll just go on my way.'' He drove down to the field and followed the trail along the fence to the river.

Moss and I stood in silence for several seconds. He glanced at me to see how I was reacting to what Elbow said. I was frowning, black clouds surrounding me.

''Doesn't look good,'' Moss said.

''No, it doesn't. His descriptions matches Aunt Iris's. The man she saw and the man that Elbow talked to is that skeleton we found.'' I took the buckle from Moss's hands and stared at it, wishing even more than ever I had let matters alone. Why did I have to be so curious? Why couldn't I let well enough alone? Not thinking what I was doing, I tossed the buckle down.

I sat on the biggest of the rocks I had been placing just before Moss came.

Moss sat beside me. He put one arm around me and took my hand in his other. "We still don't know what really happened. There could be other explanations than those you are thinking."

I shook my head. "What else could it be? Both Aunt Iris and Elbow saw the same man. Same description and same horse. Elbow even saw the buckle. Aunt Iris heard a shot. The body was killed with a Colt pistol and Gramps had such a pistol. Too many coincidences. What other explanation is there?"

Moss didn't answer as he thought it through. "But Iris said Cyrus didn't have a gun with him. That type of gun would be typical of a man from the West, not one from the Ozarks. It was probably Mr. C's gun."

Moss's giving the body a name, even an initialed one, made it even worse for me. Gramps killed a man named Mr. C! With the man's own gun, no less.

I got up and walked over to pick up the buckle. "We should tell the sheriff."

"Why? What would that accomplish except cause more grief? Cyrus Loveland has been dead for twenty years."

"Maybe Mr. C has some living relatives who would like to know what happened to him."

"Possibly. But let me do some more checking first. Knowing the town in Colorado, the date, the man's physical description, and first initial of his name, I should be able to trace him."

"Okay, but I need to tell Aunt Iris."

Moss agreed. "May I come with you again?"

"Of course." He tightened his arm around me and pulled me to him. He gave me a quick kiss.

Chapter Nine

Aunt Iris sat rigid in her chair. As Moss and I continued telling her the sheriff's conclusions, about our finding the buckle, and Elbow Jurgen's story of meeting the stranger, she held her position, betraying her anxiety by twisting the skirt of her flowered apron in her fingers. Her eyes darted back and forth from me to Moss as we each told parts of the happenings. She didn't interrupt, though her arthritic fingers worked faster as we continued. When I showed her the buckle with the large embossed C, she dropped her apron skirt, sat forward in her chair, and gave a barely audible grunt. She pressed a clenched fist to each cheek, partially covering her mouth as if forcing herself to stay silent.

When we finished, she didn't say a word. Her hands came together over her mouth and stayed there a few seconds. She slowly lowered them to the arms of her chair and then reached out to the handles of her walker. She rose from her chair with more difficulty than usual, almost as if she had given up, and scooting the walker on the linoleum floor ahead of her, started toward her bedroom.

"What's the matter, Aunt Iris?" I asked, offering to help her. Alarmed, Moss also stood up, ready to assist.

She waved aside our efforts to help, rather curtly pushing my hand from her arm, but smiling at Moss. She indicated for him to sit back down. She grabbed the handles of her walker tightly and stood as straight as she could. Her stance said plainly that here in her own house, she was still in control and, though crippled by old age and devastated by the news she just heard, she could still move around by herself, thank you very much!

"What's up?" I asked again.

"I'm okay, Darrah girl," she said softly in apology for her rudeness. "I just remembered something I need to show you. That's all."

"Let me get it for you?"

"No, I'll find it." She opened her top bureau drawer. Carelessly pushing aside several old account books and used envelopes filled with photographs, she pulled out from the back corner a yellowed flour sack tied with a faded rag strip. She held the sack out in front of her for a second. Behind her glasses her eyes were almost squinted shut as she stared at it. Its contents clanked as she dropped the bag into the tray of her walker. Her spunkiness deserted her. She swayed slightly and didn't object when I took her arm to steady her. Without a word, she returned to her chair.

Still standing where he rose, Moss stepped forward
and helped her sit back down. She allowed him to put
his hands under her arms to ease her back into the
easy chair. Then he put the walker beside her where
she could easily reach the bundle in its tray.

She looked at each of us for what seemed a long
time, but was probably only several seconds. Every
one of her eighty-eight years showed in her face and
slumped body. She sighed, untied the rag strip, which
fell apart when she tugged on it, and reached into the
cotton sack. The faded label was still visible on it. She
pulled out two silver spurs and held them out in her
trembling hand to show us. Though they badly needed
polishing to remove the tarnish, we could plainly see
a large raised C on an ornately designed background.
In a flat voice, she said, "It *was* Papa who killed the
stranger." She dropped the spurs on her tray as if they
were burning her hands. They clattered. Their leather
straps swung back and forth over the edge.

I threw my arms around her. Moss knelt beside her
and held her hand. None of us said anything. Though
we all had come to the conclusion that Cyrus Loveland
must have killed the stranger and dragged him into the
cave, no one had verbalized it with so much conviction. It was as if a jury had just given its verdict of
guilty on all counts. Like a plague, her pronouncement
polluted the air. "It was Papa who killed the
stranger."

When neither Moss nor I said anything, she said,
her eyes full of misery and shame, "We must tell the
sheriff. It's what we have to do."

"No!"

"Not yet," Moss said softly, patting her hand, which he still held. "Everything we know is circumstantial."

Aunt Iris kept shaking her head.

"At least wait until I hear from Colorado," Moss said. He stood up. "Maybe . . ."

Aunt Iris waved her open palm in front of him to stop him. "I don't see how finding out who this man was can help us in any way. I saw him, even though I convinced myself that he was a dream or something from my childish imagination. And"—she stressed the next words as if they were indisputable evidence of guilt—"Elbow saw him and *talked with him*. I heard a real gunshot. I never believed the gun was imagination. Child as I was, I sensed then that somehow an evil presence had entered our family. And I think so yet today. It scared me so that I hid and *never* told anyone. It still scares me." She indicated the spurs. "Now more than ever—"

"It was a long time ago, Aunt Iris," I interrupted. "We don't really know what . . ."

She ignored me. ". . . because now I can put together what happened. See, this is what happened. After shooting him—why my father shot him I don't know, but he did. After shooting him, then Papa kept this man's bay horse, his Colt pistol, and his silver spurs." She picked up the spurs and stared at them. "You two found his body, which fits both Elbow's and my memories of him, and, more than that, you found a belt buckle matching the spurs from the skeleton that will surely identify him." She clamped her lips tight and, nodding her head, said in a tone that allowed no contradiction, "My father killed him."

I expected her to go to pieces as she did when Gramps died. Then Abby and other relatives had had to stay with her for a couple of weeks before she was herself again. But now her emotions showed only through her horror-filled eyes, which stared at the set of spurs she held in a thin hand that trembled so much she had to use both to keep them steady.

"Where did you get these?" I asked, taking them from her. I shot a glance at Moss who was comparing the design on the spurs to that of the silver buckle. They were identical.

"Papa gave them to me when he gave Arnie the pistol. He said they were both keepsakes from his western days and he wanted us, his two oldest, to have them."

"Did he say anything else about them?" I asked. "Like how come the initial was a C instead of L for Loveland?"

"Not about the letter. I didn't think anything about it. I assumed it stood for Cyrus." She looked at Moss. "But a man wouldn't use his first initial, would he?"

"No."

"Anything else, Aunt Iris? Think."

She looked at me as she used to when I was a little girl and didn't show the proper respect for an older person. With her customary spirit returning to her voice, she said, "I may be crippled with rheumatism, Darrah girl, but I still have my mind." She looked at Moss as if he and she were in a conspiracy together to put up with me.

She pushed herself erect in her chair. "I remember well when he gave them to us, because he singled me out from the boys. It was unusual for him to give man stuff like this to a daughter, even if she was the oldest. I was really honored that he would think of me on the same terms as his sons." She covered her mouth with her hand as she remembered something else. "He told me to keep these spurs safe because someday they might be valuable."

"Like worth lots of money?" Moss asked.

She nodded. "That's what I thought. Pure silver work, you know. They must be worth lots of money. I'd almost forgotten about them. When I moved my things from the farm to this house, I remember I put them in the back of the drawer to give to you, Darrah girl, when you got older because you like horses and were closer to Papa than any of the others of your generation."

"But now," Moss asked, "what do you think he meant by them being valuable?"

"Because they're evidence covering up his past," she said with no visible emotion.

"If he had wanted to cover up what he did, he wouldn't have saved them or given them to you. He'd have thrown them away," Moss said.

"Yes," Aunt Iris said, her backbone stiff again. "That seems likely."

"Or he would have left them on the body in the cave," I said.

"So why did he save them, and the gun, and make such a production out of giving them to you and your brother?" Moss asked.

Aunt Iris's voice was so faint I could barely hear her. "I don't know. It doesn't make much sense. Except it wasn't in his nature to leave them to rust away in the cave. He couldn't bear to see anything wasted. I guess he took off of the stranger some of the reusable things."

"What about his hat? Did Gramps ever have a big cowboy hat?" I doubted it because a picture of him in a cowboy hat would be as inane as Julius Caesar wearing one.

"No."

"Or jeans or boots that he normally wouldn't wear?" Moss asked.

"Not that I remember. Just the gun and spurs."

"And both of them are durable and can be traced back to the guy from the West that you and Elbow saw. Don't you think it strange that he kept those incriminating items?"

"I don't know, young man, I just don't know." Her head dropped to the right as her hands clasped the padded arms of her chair. "Perhaps he wanted us to find out someday."

"Why would he want that?" I asked.

"Maybe to clear his conscience? Be forgiven? I don't know. He always had a reputation for being an honest man. It doesn't make any sense. None of this is like him. He was such a gentle person, loved his family and animals. Forever planting some flowering tree or plant."

Tears formed in Aunt Iris's eyes. She fumbled in the pocket of her apron and brought out a handkerchief. She wiped her face and clasped the handkerchief in her hand for future use. "Here, Darrah girl," she said, handing me the empty flour sack and pushing the spurs closer to me, "you keep the spurs. I don't want to see them ever again."

"Does your brother still have the gun?" Moss asked.

"He's dead these thirty years."

"Did he give it to Abby or her brother?" I asked. Turning to Moss I said, "They are his children."

"I don't know. I never heard of it again, but I'll call Abby and ask her." She brightened up when she realized there was something she could do to help us with our investigation. "Can they tell if the bullet they found in the skeleton's spine came from that gun?" she asked Moss. "I've seen them match them up on television shows all the time."

"I think so," he said.

Aunt Iris nodded and punched in Abby's quick-dial number on the telephone on the end table beside her.

"Abby, dear, yes, I'm fine. Listen, I've got something to ask you. Darrah is here with Moss Wright. Yes, I remember you told me he bought the home place. No, I don't think they are." She looked up at Moss and me, put her hand over the mouthpiece, and whispered to us, "She thinks you two are . . ." She didn't finish, but we knew what she meant. Then speaking back into the phone, "No, Abby, he is here about some business about the farm. You know, the landscaping that Darrah is doing on the home place. And he's interested in old guns, especially pistols." She crossed her fingers and held them up to us to cover her fib. "And I just told him about that old Colt pistol that my father gave Arnie back when he finished high school. He would like to see it if it's still in the family.''

As Abby talked, Aunt Iris shook her head at us. Because we were there, she was able to hang up without the usual long conversation.

"She didn't know anything about it. And that means that Arnie disposed of it before Abby was old enough to remember.'' She sighed. "I don't know if I'm glad or not.''

"I'm glad," I said. "Matching up to that gun would have given us positive proof Gramps did it.''

"Not necessarily,'' Moss said. "Proof of that gun being the murder weapon, but not that Cyrus pulled the trigger. We don't know. His having a Colt could be a coincidence. Colts were rather common guns.''

Aunt Iris and I both knew that he was trying to lessen our fears. We were sure that the gun was the murder weapon, whether we could produce it or not. Elbow saw a pistol on the stranger. That was proof enough for us. There were too many coincidences for it not to be true.

"I'm sorry, Moss," Aunt Iris said, "for lying to Abby about your gun collection. If I didn't give some reason for asking, Abby would suspect something.''

"That's all right. I do like guns and have a few, so you didn't lie.''

Aunt Iris smiled for the first time since we showed her the belt buckle. "I figured you did. Like to hunt as well as fish?''

"Yes. That's another reason I bought the farm.''

"The Loveland men all love to fish and hunt. Some

of the women, too. I never hunted, but I used to fish a lot. Papa loved to hunt—quail, rabbits, small game. But in Colorado he hunted big game, deer, elk, and mountain lions. He told us lots of stories about his adventures.'' She turned to Moss. ''That was back when there weren't any deer around here and before they were restocked. Darrah tells me there are deer on the farm now.''

Even though Aunt Iris didn't have advance warning of us coming to visit her this time, she served us oatmeal cookies and spice tea. As we left, she said to Moss, ''You didn't know what you were getting into when you bumped into us in our old driveway, did you?''

Moss held her hand and patted it. ''Not then, but now I know. Two lovely women. That's what I found.''

''And a dead body,'' I said.

Moss didn't answer.

On our way back to Timberton, I was miserable as I sat beside Moss in his pickup. I didn't know how to react to having a murderer in my family. Finding the spurs settled all of my lingering doubts. One by one pieces of evidence were piling up to the incontestable fact that my cherished great-grandfather was a murderer. The black mood I felt when I first saw the wasted homestead returned even blacker with the ruin of my family's proud name. The shame was there, even if only Aunt Iris and I knew. And Moss, of course. If only he hadn't dug that blasted lake!

I glanced at him. His brows were tightened in concentration as he drove down the highway, watching out for the increased traffic of late afternoon. From hating him thoroughly for destroying the buildings, I had come almost a complete circle around to not only liking him, but letting him share this dark secret.

He probably knew I was staring at him, though he didn't take his eyes from the highway to look back. His head was held erect so that I saw his profile. His brown hair fell loosely on his high forehead. His perfectly formed nose led to his full lips above a firm chin. No flab there or on his tanned neck. I could hardly believe that less than three weeks ago, I didn't know he existed.

"There must be some explanation," he said. "From what you and Iris tell me about Cyrus, I don't think he could have killed anyone. Someone else could have been there that Iris didn't see. She was just a kid and might not remember things exactly right. Cyrus may not have had anything to do with Mr. C at all. Someone else killed him. Perhaps a neighbor who knew about the deserted spring cave and dumped him there."

"But the guy knew Gramps. He asked Elbow directions to his place."

"That is a problem."

"And what about the spurs and gun?"

"Maybe they fell off the murdered guy and Cyrus found them. Maybe the murderer planted them there to frame Cyrus in case the body was discovered."

"And the bay horse?"

"There are lots of bay horses. Probably the most common color. Iris said Cyrus traded horses all the time."

"But the name, Goldie?"

"Could mean anything. It's a good name for a horse. Maybe Iris got it mixed up with some other horse. How many horses did Cyrus own?"

"In his lifetime?"

Moss nodded.

"Gee, I don't know. Hundreds, probably. I remember a couple of dozen myself." I was feeling better.

"So, let's hold off judgment until we find real proof." On a stretch with no traffic, he looked at me with his full-blown smile. "It's not the end of the world. Think of it as our private mystery. More than just landscaping my place, we are together on this. You and I. A real whodunit." He looked at the road and slowed down when the school bus ahead of us signaled it would turn off.

I had to admit that being together appealed to me. His lighter tone reassured me. In spite of myself, I grinned.

"That's the way," he said. "You, me, and your Aunt Iris, we are the Three Musketeers. Capes flapping in the wind of circumstantial evidence, swords out in defiance of our doubts, we march on, despairing not, to protect the honor of the Loveland family patriarch."

I laughed at the image of Aunt Iris in breeches and boots wearing a big hat with a feather flowing behind.

"That's better," he said. He reached out his arm to pull me closer to him. "Now we'll just have to be patient and wait while I try to find out some more information about Mr. C. I've contacted some people in Goldfield, Colorado, who are looking through old records.''

We drove the rest of the way back to town with his left arm on my shoulder. The warmth of his leg touching mine alleviated some of my misery.

Chapter Ten

The next Saturday I was again sitting beside Moss, only this time in his Chrysler convertible on our way to an isolated rock shut-in formation in eastern Missouri. The weather was balmy for early October; the warm breeze blew my hair as the sun's rays made my freckles pop out more than ever. With his cap bill pulled down close to his eyes, Moss looked and acted more like a kid than the CEO of Moss Industries.

His eyes took in every picturesque barn, every orange sassafras tree, each dead tree trunk clothed with scarlet Virginia creeper or poison ivy, and the masses of magenta sumac that lined the curvy highway. This was an area of the Ozarks he had never seen. We were on a daylong excursion, his first in many months of steady work with the new addition to his plant. During the entire three-hour drive he kept up a never-ending stream of questions and exclamations.

"Just look at that color in the woods! So many dif-

ferent plants. Isn't that rock formation over there granite? I've seen only sedimentary rock around our area.
Why are azaleas native here and not at home?'' Getting some seeds from the wild azaleas to plant along
his brooklet was the reason for our trip.

With frequent interruptions when he spotted some
sight or plant he wanted me to see, I explained again
that the main geological difference here from our area
was that in places here the granite was exposed, and
because of the more acid soil, there were native azaleas growing wild along some of the streams. In our
area the limestone rocks formed eons ago over the
underlying granite made the soil too alkaline for azaleas to grow wild. However, we could grow them well
if we prepared the soil before we planted them.

Back at the Loveland farm during the past week,
we had almost completed the work immediately
around the lake and along the branch. A soft green
velvet already covered the bare earthen dam and the
seeded areas around the lake. Young trees arranged in
groves and placed artistically around the area, as well
as bushes, ferns, and ground cover, gave structure and
dimension to the former emptiness. A pebbled drive
curved gracefully from the entranceway across the rustic bridge to the tall walnut trees at the edge of the
bluff hill, urging the visitor to enter, loiter, and enjoy.
It was all beginning to come together.

The lake was brimming with springwater that sparkled in the autumn sun and rippled in the breeze. The
day I telephoned Moss that the water was lapping
against the rocky spillway ready to flow out, he rushed
out to witness the birth of his spring branch—the first

overflow from the lake. He arrived in time to see the headwater hug the rocks of the falls while it filled every little hole and crevice as it gathered into a little pool and then dropped over the falls. After it recovered from the fall and filled the scooped-out basin, we watched it creep along the path we'd created for it, disappear under the bridge, and soon reappear on the other side. From there on, its pace was a little faster as it tumbled downhill.

It was time to celebrate. How many people can witness the birth of a spring-fed brook? Allen and Carl whooped and struck their shovels against each other. That seemed to them to be an appropriate celebratory sign that suited the occasion.

Connie could hardly contain herself. "We did it!" She shook everyone's hand and pounded me on the back. She said it with amazement, as if she hadn't thought we could. Then she looked at me and let out a big sigh. I knew then how trying my attitude had been on her. She was constantly afraid I would still do something to ruin this job.

"Yes, Connie, we did," I said. My shoulders relaxed and the knot I'd held in my stomach eased. I hadn't been sure I could stick it through either. I put my arm over her shoulder. Together we looked over the entrance area. What a difference! The change was not just from the earlier bulldozed-out starkness, but from the scene engraved in my mind from my great-grandparents' time. The present beauty and the promise of greater richness when the plants matured overshadowed my waning feeling of loss. Connie and

I had captured an aura, or a presence, that was merely a suggestion during the Loveland era.

Moss, impatient with the slow progress of the water, grabbed me by my hand. Running, he pulled me back up the brook to the spillway, as if to assure himself that the source would continue to feed the brook or that the flow wouldn't just disappear into the ground. An unending flow poured over the spillway. From that higher position he watched the roll of water push steadily on, pulled by gravity toward the river. It turned exactly where we wanted it to, filled little pools where we planned, and tumbled over or around boulders we placed in its way. The undertone of running water joined the sighing of the breeze and the occasional call of a mourning dove. Enjoying the beauty and peace in the combination of nature and our creativity, I forgot for a moment the scents of death buried in the lake water . . . the Loveland family buildings . . . and Mr. C.

"It's absolutely perfect!" Moss said, hugging me as he gave a thumbs-up sign to the others. "Just perfect." He ran down the stream again, pausing at the bridge. "All it needs are some azaleas bushes right about here."

"No problem," I said. I wondered why I hadn't thought of them myself. A bank of them would highlight April and May viewing.

"But I don't want exotic plants," he said, "just native ones."

"There are native azaleas in the Ozarks. Most people call them honeysuckle bushes. They grow wild in areas that have a more acid soil than we have here."

"Really? Can you get some?" The little-boy eagerness came to his eyes.

"That's easy," I said. I'd been wanting to get some native azaleas for our nursery. Here was the chance.

Getting a start on these azaleas was the reason that we were making the trip in his convertible. When I told him I knew a place where we could get some seed—and it was the perfect time of year for gathering—he set up the next Saturday for the trip. He didn't ask me to go; he just assumed that I would. He was right. I wanted to go, not only to get the seed for his landscaping and more for Connie and me to start some plants in our nursery, but because I welcomed spending a whole day with him. The trip wasn't exactly a date, just an extension of our working relationship. But it felt like a date.

Back at his place the day the lake overflowed, he had been so keyed up about the new brook that he almost forgot to tell me the results of his research into Mr. C in Goldfield.

While the others were busy elsewhere, he said to me, "I think that the murdered man's name was Lem Cowan. At least I think that he is the one because first, his name begins with a C, and second, Cyrus's name and his are linked on a record in the gold-mining area. He's probably the one."

The information he found confirmed what we already suspected, but shed no light on why this man came to the Loveland farm, or why he was killed and dragged into the spring cave.

According to what Moss found out, in September 1919 Cyrus Loveland and Lem Cowan filed jointly on a mineral claim near Goldfield, Colorado. Moss found no other information on Cowan, though Loveland's home address was recorded. A record dated January 23, 1920, showed that Loveland exchanged gold nuggets for $5,000. No mention of Cowan. Moss put Cowan's name through every search agent he knew without finding any other trace of him. However, he found several records of Cyrus back in Missouri—the census, inheritance of his farm from his father, taxes, marriage, a mention or two in the local paper, death notice, and probate records of his will. Except for the one entry as a partner with Cyrus, it was as if Lem Cowan never existed.

"No wonder no one ever came looking for him," I said. "He had no family."

"He could have been using an alias," Moss said.

After a telephone conversation with Aunt Iris, we three decided that we could do no more. Without further evidence, we agreed to leave the mystery alone. Both Aunt Iris and I had calmed down, and looking at it from the eighty-year perspective, with Moss's convincing arguments that we couldn't be sure Cyrus had anything to do with the murder, we decided we should think positive.

"Keep his memory as you knew him," Moss said. "That's the real man as far as you two are concerned."

"He's right, Darrah girl," Iris said. Once again, as always, like coping with the loss of all of her immediate family and the destruction of the home buildings, she knew how to accept whatever happened and go on living. I hadn't learned that yet. Even though she could return Gramps to his pedestal, I couldn't do it so easily. I wasn't strong enough to put him back up.

"Yes, Aunt Iris, I know he's right." I said the words but didn't really believe them. I couldn't forget the skeleton we found. Doubts seeped into my thoughts without my permission. For instance, if the two men were partners, how come Cyrus was the only one cashing in the gold? Or if the five thousand dollars was half the gold they mined, then why wasn't Cowan's record there too? (I was glad to put a name to him. I didn't like the Mr. C label. It seemed too friendly or intimate.)

Did Gramps steal their complete take? If he did, then Cowan might have followed him to Missouri for his share. Aunt Iris said Gramps ran right up to him, as if he knew him, and Elbow said the man was looking for Gramps. The two men argued out there in the driveway. Was their dispute about Cowan's half of the money? By this time even if he had wanted to, Gramps couldn't have given Cowan half of the money because Gramps had already spent it on his house and barn.

Although to my mind these new doubts seemed to point even more directly to Gramps, I forced myself to shut them out. Both Moss and Iris seemed willing to let the mystery lie, to go on as if we hadn't discovered a murdered body. So should I. There were more important things going on now, such as Magic Landscaping's dream job and the man who hired us to do it. There was this trip to the shut-ins with Moss to collect wild azalea seeds. *Enjoy the present,* I told myself. *Don't let what Gramps may or may not have done ruin the potential of a wonderful day with Moss.*

All of these memories and thoughts were racing through my mind as we drove through southern Missouri. I didn't notice the miles flying by. I didn't listen carefully to Moss's running commentary or to his last question.

"Moss to Darrah, come in please," he said, laughing at my preoccupation and touching me lightly on my knee.

"Uh! What did you say?"

"I asked, just what are shut-ins?" he repeated. "I know it doesn't refer to an old folks' home, but why is a rock formation called a shut-in?"

"It's a gorge where the stream has cut through and between granite knobs. It's an area where the stream cannot spread out into a valley as usually happens in the Ozarks, therefore the term 'shut-in.' The channel of the stream is literally shut in, forced to flow between granite walls."

Moss's frown showed that he still didn't understand. "On the Loveland farm, for instance," I explained, "the river flows through sedimentary rock—limestone and sandstone—and has eroded out a wide valley, creating the bottomlands. Here, where these knobs of resistant granite are exposed, the river is forced into a narrow channel because granite is too hard for the water to erode away."

"You certainly know a lot about the area," Moss said. "Did you study it in school?"

"No. I just picked it up. Mostly from Gramps. He talked a lot about rocks as well as plants."

To get to the Rocky Oak Shut-Ins that I knew about where the wild azaleas grew, we had to hike in a couple of miles. The first part of the hike was along the creek valley that was similar to our river valley. Then the trail curved around a side of Stone Pile Mountain, a jumble of granite that rose above the trail. When we reached the shut-ins, jagged, pink granite rocks closed in on either side of the creek as if to block the creek's flow. When the creek reached the rocks, the water separated into several channels, tumbling over granite slabs and diverting rounded boulders worn smooth from centuries of water erosion.

"Why doesn't the creek just go around these rocks?" Moss asked. The whole shut-ins area covered only a few acres.

"I don't know." Viewed from a distance, it looked as if the water could make a slight detour to avoid the rocks. "I guess the water is determined to have its way, working harder to go straight through than taking the easier way around."

Moss smiled. "Like you butting up against this Cowan man's skeleton? The easiest way would be to go around what you've discovered. Leave it alone. But you push right through the center, hurting yourself the farther in that you go."

"But . . ."

"I know you told Iris you'd let it go, but you haven't. You're going to keep eroding away at that hard stone until you break through."

He was too much on the mark for me to be comfortable about the conversation. I was afraid, when I did manage to break through, that I would find even more ugliness and evil, not the peace and beauty created by the shut-ins. Since Moss started the metaphor,

I continued it, attempting to cover my fears. "But see all this beauty that the water has achieved by pushing through the hard way? Without the creek these wonderful rocks would be hidden." I saw no way that this metaphor could be extended to cover my great-grandfather. No beauty could come from a murder.

"It's awesome," Moss agreed. Then he said aloud what I was thinking. "But what you discover may not be so pleasant."

The results of the creek's labor opened up before us. On either side of the gorge, slick, almost perpendicular bluffs entrapped the current that spilled over and around smoothed slabs and rounded boulders of pinkish granite. Behind the shut-ins and framing the gorge were russet and orange oaks and red and yellow maples. The colors were mirrored upside down in the calmer water pool at the foot of the ravine.

With one deep exclamation of pleasure at the view, Moss dropped his backpack and jumped from rock to rock, not worrying that his sneakers were getting wet. From our side, it was easy to walk down the sloping rocks to the water's edge, that is, if we watched our footing. Without following him, I watched him hop to the other side. There the granite rose up about twenty feet in an almost perpendicular wall.

Moss started climbing the wall! He had no rope. I couldn't see any indentations for him to hold on to, though they obviously were there, for he made steady progress up the cliff. With careful placing of his hands and lifting one foot at a time, he started scaling the wall like Spider-Man. His rust-red jacket and black jeans even helped create the illusion of a spider.

"Moss!" I yelled at him. I was trembling. I'm not too good at heights. Deepwater and even underwater caves don't scare me, but sheer heights do. What if he slipped and fell? We were two miles from the car. We hadn't passed any house since we stopped a ways back to ask the owner permission to hike in and gather some seeds. If Moss got in trouble, no way could I get him to help.

My heart jumped. I pushed my hair from my eyes. A shower of pebbles and dirt tumbled down as a little bush he was holding on to gave way. He turned his grinning face to me and shouted, "No problem." As he held on securely to a crag with his other hand, he held out the bush and, with a dramatic gesture, let it drop. It fell to the smooth, water-covered boulders below him. It splashed, swirled once, and was carried downstream by the rushing waters.

"Be careful!" I shouted back.

"Piece of cake," he yelled, still grinning. Then I realized he had pulled out the sprout on purpose to impress me.

He continued slowly, and more carefully, up the cliff. As he got higher, the climb became more difficult; the distance down to the rocks below was much greater. He had difficulty finding secure handholds. Two other times he knocked down dirt or pebbles to clean out a hold that would support himself.

I couldn't understand why I was so afraid for him, unless he meant much more to me than I admitted. Just when it seemed that he had it made, his left foot slipped as he tried to place it a few inches higher. For a moment his foot dangled in the air. All that held him on the cliff above the boulders and rushing water were his fingers gripping a crevice I couldn't see and a slight toehold with his right foot on what looked like a solid cliff wall. This time he wasn't faking it. His expression showed that he was in trouble.

"Moss!" I yelled again. Even during my fright, or perhaps because of it, I noticed three buzzards circling lazily above, their wings spread out to catch the air drafts.

The toe of his left sneaker found a niche. He cautiously put it in to test if it would hold him. After some more gravel bounced off the cliff, he put his weight in the indentation. It held. First his right hand and then his left reached up and seemed to stick to the bare rock surface. Then he lifted his right foot which was sustaining most of his weight. By now he was high enough to reach over the edge and grab a small, solidly rooted tree trunk. Only then did he turn his face toward me with a big smile.

"No sweat!" I think he said. As high up as he was and over the roar of the water and the beating of my heart, it was difficult to hear. I let out my breath when he pulled himself over the rim and sat down, his feet swinging back and forth over the edge. He lifted both arms in the air and shook them. "Yahoo!" I heard his voice distinctly this time as he gave the yell. The gorge wasn't deep enough for sounds to echo. His jubilant tone merged with the breeze and water, and lost itself in the forest behind him.

He poised there on the edge of the cliff, admiring the view for a few minutes. Weak-kneed, I sat down on my smooth, flat boulder, safely on ground level.

Without realizing it, I had held myself rigid during his entire climb. I relaxed my shoulders. During that second when he hung perilously over the gorge, I knew that he meant much more to me than I had been willing to admit.

After resting a few minutes, he rose and waved to me. I was half afraid that he was going to climb back down the way he went up, but he disappeared into the trees behind him. At the north end of the shut-ins, where the rocks ended and the creek entered a little valley, I saw him come out from the line of trees and jump onto a boulder in the water. But instead of crossing and returning to me along the path, he took the water route, zigzagging back and forth, leaping from boulder to boulder, some several feet high, until he was directly across from me. Between us was a chasm of rushing water, just one of the many channels the creek had to take to get through.

"C'mon, jump," he said, holding out his arms to catch me. The distance was about three feet. On solid, level ground I could easily jump that. He kept motioning for me to come. What the heck! Why not?

I laid my backpack on the creek bank beside Moss's, made sure that I was standing on a dry spot so I wouldn't slip, and jumped. I landed in his arms, my momentum making him stagger a bit. He plopped down into a sitting position still holding me. I was clasping him tightly to keep from falling off the narrow perch we were on. I landed on his lap. With both of us laughing, he hugged me.

No one was in sight. Since we hadn't seen anyone on our hike there, we knew we were alone in this

fantastic natural wonderland. It seemed perfectly normal that we kiss and I stay in his arms. A whippoor-
will called behind us. Another answered across the
creek. A bullfrog gave erratic croaks while the rhythm
of the falling, foaming water never ceased.

"From up there on the bluff looking down at you,
Darrah, you looked like a flower. Your green slacks
were the stem. When you spread out your arms to
wave to me, they were the leaves, and your red hair
was the flower. Kind of like a rose." He put his hand
on my chin and looked into my eyes. He ran his other
hand over my short hair. "Like the bud of a red rose
just ready to open."

I laughed. "When I was born and Gramps saw my
red hair, he tried unsuccessfully to get my parents to
call me Rose. He had named all his girls for flowers.
Iris, Pansy, Lily, and Daisy." I remembered his pet
name for me. "He often called me his Red Rose."

"Good name. It suits you. You sure looked like a
little red rose from the cliff." He paused, still looking
at me. "I wish I'd known him," Moss said.

"Yeah, me too. He'd have liked you. It's funny how
a lot of memories are coming back. I hadn't thought
of that nickname in years."

We watched as a mother wood duck and eight or
ten babies swam into view in the quiet pool at the end
of the shut-in formation. Moss had pointed out an eagle perched on a dead oak tree farther down the
stream. Suddenly the eagle dive-bombed at the little
family of ducks. The mother duck flapped her wings.
We were too far away to hear her squawking. The little
ones dived under the water. The eagle missed when

the babies went under. He circled up and tried again. Same result. When he zoomed down to the surface of the water, the ducks had all disappeared, only to re-surface when the eagle flew off.

"Will eagles come to my lake?" Moss asked.

"Probably."

Moss hugged me in delight.

It was later in the afternoon when we found the azalea bushes that were loaded with seed. We gathered what we needed and with arms around each other, walked slowly back to the road and Moss's car parked over to the side. We got an unexpected bonus when we stopped back at the owner's house to thank him. He took us to an overgrown area behind his building that he was going to clear, telling us to dig up any azalea bushes we wanted. We took all we could squeeze into Moss's trunk. Thrilled that we now had instant bushes, instead of having to wait several years for the plants to grow from seed, we headed home. It had been a perfect day!

Chapter Eleven

The wonderful day wasn't over. Full of our stay at the shut-ins, pleased with the seeds and plants we gathered, and our growing attraction for each other, we welcomed the three hours of driving ahead of us to return home. No beepers, no interruptions. Just Moss and I.

I hate the front seats of cars now. With the console between the driver and passenger, there was no way Moss and I could sit close together. When he didn't need both hands for driving, he put his hand on my knee or he held my hand.

On our drive to the shut-ins we had talked about the work on his farm, which was progressing well; Magic Landscaping was ready to enter the next phase of our plans, landscaping the bench land and bluff areas bordering the lake region. Our research about Lem Cowan had reached an impasse; we knew of no other means of discovering what had happened. Going home we talked about ourselves.

The trip was another milestone in our relationship. Finding the skeleton together while scuba diving had already moved us beyond client/landscaper arrangements; the trip let us learn about each other. Like the new grass seeded around the lake, our friendship was growing. We were discovering much about each other. During the drive home we shared life histories.

Raised in a condo in Philadelphia, Moss relished from boyhood the camping and hiking trips he made to the mountains. He participated in other outdoor activities—rock climbing, bicycling, swimming, snorkeling, fishing, and hunting. A biology teacher in the ninth grade made him aware of plants. On his outings from the city, he began his collection of leaves, bark, and fruit of as many different plants as he could find.

His maternal grandparents developed Moss Industries. He was their only descendant. From childhood he was groomed to go into the business and eventually take over. At first, he was not sure management was what he wanted to do. In his first apprentice assignments in the East he did well, but didn't have his heart in it, though he realized he was getting valuable leadership experience. After a few promotions in the company's plants in Philadelphia and Baltimore, his grandfather put him in charge of building, opening, and operating the small factory in Timberton.

As with his other responsibilities, he did a good job of setting up the new plant. At first it was only an assignment until he became more familiar with the region. As his interest in the area grew, so did his enthusiasm about his job.

He was excited that the outdoor activities he loved were available without his having to travel many miles. He could take his choice of any, all within a twenty-mile radius. And to add to his pleasure, he found more species of native plants than he had ever found together in one area. He located most of the plants he knew about from the East, as well as a myriad of prairie plants, desertlike plants on the rocky glades, swamp plants along the sloughs of the rivers, and arcticlike plants along springs from north-facing bluffs. He spent every spare moment hiking, biking, and floating the river to add to his collection.

Then he discovered the Loveland farm. On a float trip down our river, his party camped for the night on the gravel bar under the swinging bridge. Before dark, and early the next morning before the group broke camp, he hiked up the bluff and found the caves, with a spring flowing from the biggest one. He was amazed at the many species of plants he saw, some he wasn't familiar with.

Later, learning that the unoccupied farm was for sale, he drove back to explore the whole farm, first alone, and then with the realtor. The place had every natural feature that he wanted, as well as great possibilities for improvement. He purchased the farm. His first improvement (his word not mine) was to tear down the old, deteriorating buildings that were located on the most favorable spot on the whole place for constructing a lake. If later he wanted to build, he located the perfect site for a house up on the bluff with a view of the woods, river, and valley.

By this time, I had become inured to thinking of the farm without the buildings. I didn't squirm when Moss told of building his lake as if destroying the house was nothing more than removing an objectionable pile of rocks.

His interest in the new factory in Timberton increased with his delight with his farm. The plant prospered. Moss took advantage of its central location and access to Interstate 44 and the availability of a skilled labor pool. Within a year he convinced the board of directors to expand.

"At first buying the farm was just an investment," Moss told me. "But the more I learn about it, the more I like it. I've decided I will settle here. I don't know if I will live on the farm, but I know that I want to stay in the area. My grandfather is agreeable to that. He's planning on retiring in a couple of years when he thinks I'm ready to take over as president. When that happens we are planning to move our main offices here."

He squeezed my hand as he smiled at me. "Now I have the best reason yet to stick around."

A warm glow spread over me.

I told him about myself, how Connie and I joined up and about our business. How we were growing steadily with plans for more greenhouses to propagate unusual and rare native plants. We realized from the start that the local area alone could not support our nursery output. We had just initiated a mail-order branch and developed a Web site on the Internet. Early results from both of these outlets were promising. Now we were reaching out all over the country. From the beginning with just the two of us doing all the work, we now used ten employees during the busy seasons.

As usual whenever I found anyone patient enough to listen to my ramblings, I started gabbing about my family, a broad topic by itself. I usually have to limit myself or I'll bore my listeners. I'd worn Connie out long ago. If I even mentioned to her something about the Lovelands, she would groan and roll back her head. I'd learned to keep what I said short. But Moss seemed genuinely interested, asking questions to encourage me to tell more. It was natural that I talked a lot about Gramps. He was of interest to both of us. Ever since Aunt Iris and I first sighted the farm without the buildings, Gramps was often in my thoughts. Finding the skeleton and suspecting Gramps only intensified my recollections.

After sharing our stories, our talk returned to our successful day. Moss was still excited about scaling the cliff at the shut-ins. Somehow his way of describing his experience to me reminded me of one of Gramps's stories about the rock climbing he did in Colorado. From Gramps's stories, it seemed that he tackled anything. He described one adventure after another about his time in the West.

I was reminded of one particular time when he and his partner scaled a cliff to find a shorter route to their claim instead of hiking miles up a winding, mountainous creek. Just like what happened to Moss, Gramps's foot slipped when he was almost at the top of the cliff. I played the story over in my mind. Gramps said that he dangled in the air, two hundred feet high, holding on to a dead tree trunk. As he thrashed around, his partner looked down on him from the top and laughed. At first Gramps lost one handhold on the tree and his thrashing feet scraped against the smooth rock surface before one boot found a niche solid enough to hold him.

Suddenly I sat forward in my seat. Other stories of Gramps's scrolled through my mind. As if I had typed PARTNER and clicked SEARCH on a computer, two specific tales appeared. I could hear Gramps's voice telling them.

"He said *partner*," I said out loud. "I remember that he said *partner*."

"What? Who said it?" Moss was startled by my sudden movement.

Poor Moss. He didn't know what I was thinking or why his story made me remember something. "My great-grandfather. I just remembered a couple of his stories where he mentioned a *partner*."

Moss was immediately interested. Lem Cowan and Gramps were partners, according to Moss's research. From the change in my mood, he could tell I had something important to say. "Tell me."

"The family all thought that most of what Gramps said was what he made up, or at least that he greatly exaggerated the truth. The others groaned when he started to repeat one of his stories. I was the only one who listened. He told his tales in the first person, but we knew he didn't do all the things he said he did. Usually he had all those adventures by himself. But this one story, when he almost fell off a cliff, he spoke of a partner.''

''What did the partner do?''

''Nothing. That's the funny thing about it. I think that was part of the reason he told it. He and his partner climbed a cliff. The partner got to the top first. When Gramps got into trouble his partner didn't help him. I think the partner would have let him fall to his death.''

Moss listened eagerly. ''This may be important to help us link Cyrus to Cowan. Do you remember any other stories when he mentioned a partner?''

Moss remained quiet while I concentrated. I was just a little kid. I sorted out the jumble of memories in my mind trying to bring back the mood. I was sitting in the gently rocking porch swing beside Gramps. I made myself feel again the softness of his pale blue, chambray shirtsleeve against my neck when he put his arm over my shoulder to emphasize some dramatic place in his story. I could feel the stiff thickness of his overalls against my bare leg. Level with my eyes was the raised circle his watch made in the bib pocket.

I remembered more details of the two stories.

''You remember something, don't you?'' Moss asked. When he could take his eyes from the road, he shot quick glances at me.

''Yes. There were two other stories he told that had a partner in them, but they weren't about him. He told them about some other man he met.''

''Tell me anyway.''

''In the last year of his life he repeated a lot of stuff. I bet I heard these stories a dozen times. Probably another reason I remember them is because, even as a kid, I wondered why they were so important to him when they weren't even about him. I'd tell him he had already told them to me, you know, like kids do, but he'd go right on. 'This is important,' he'd say. 'Listen good.' "

"Did he say that about all the stories he told, or just certain ones?"

I didn't remember for sure. "No, I think just certain ones."

"Okay, tell me those, and especially those with a partner."

As I quickly ran the stories through my mind, the dark mood I'd worn since first sighting the lake suddenly left me. I sat back in my seat, my face beaming. The world was bright again. At that moment I knew. Here we had been looking everywhere for clues to the murder and Gramps's involvement in it, when all along I was the one who held the key to what happened. He had told me. Over and over.

Moss took quick glances at my smiling face while driving across a river valley and heading up a long curvy hill. "Tell me," he said again.

I nodded, but paused a few seconds to better organize my thoughts. I'm not a bad storyteller myself. Inherited it, I suspect. Or learned the knack from an expert, more likely. I couldn't resist the dramatic opportunity to take center front stage. Like Gramps, I would entertain Moss while disclosing what I just figured out. It was what Gramps made sure that I knew, even though I didn't understand what I was supposed to know. Until now.

"We were sitting on the porch, Gramps and I, the swing squeaking as we rocked back and forth." I started squeezing Moss's hand. " 'Now you listen good, Red Rose,' Gramps said, jerking on my one long braid at the back of my neck. Though he had been grinning and teasing me about a boy I liked, he suddenly became serious. His farsighted eyes looked out over his front yard and down the drive to the gate. 'Listen good, my little Red Rose,' he said."

I paused a few seconds. "This is the story he told."

There was these here two fellers, partners, who had slaved on their claim fer several months. They had panned out some gold. No bonanza, mind you, but by workin' hard they got enough that the one feller from back East was satisfied with his share. He wanted to cash it in, take his half, and go home to his wife and kiddies. He missed 'em somethin' terrible.

His partner wasn't so inclined. He wanted more, and being dilatory himself, he needed the feller from the East to stay and help since he was the one that done most of the work. He wanted them to go farther back up the mountain to stake out another claim where he heard they was good pickin's. Now, Charlie, the feller I'm tellin' about, Charlie knowed that their claim was all worked out, and he didn't want to look nowheres else. All he wanted was to go home.

So one evenin' Charlie announces that he'd be goin' to the assayer's office the next day to turn his share of the gold into money. The partner, Lou—that was his name, Lou—ain't about to let him go. He grabs the bag of gold and starts runnin' back up the creek away from their camp.

'Course, Charlie hightails it after him. There was all the gold from his half year's work a-disappearin' right afore him. Now, he'd been a-watchin' Lou fer some time to make sure he didn't run off with it. Never trusted him, one of them fellers that's narrow between the eyes, you know? They'd been a few times when Charlie seen that Lou a-tryin' to steal the bag of gold. Lou was mean, too, even fixin' up his horse's bridle with one of them wicked spade bits so that his horse's mouth bled. Charlie couldn't abide no cruelty to animals.

So he is ready for Lou to do somethin' like takin' the gold. He is ten years younger, and he soon catches up to Lou. They git into a big ruckus. Charlie lights into him, tackles him. They fall to the ground. Lou loses his hold on the sack, and it rolls down the slope a ways until it bumps into a big rock. It was tied tight with rawhide, so none of the gold nuggets spilled out, and the bag was strong leather.

First Charlie is on top and a-poundin' away on Lou. They are a-swearin' and a-cussin'. Then Lou gives a big lunge and knocks Charlie off. Lou rolls over and, still layin' on the ground, pulls out his gun. "Don't you come one step closer," he yells at Charlie, who bounces up and is about to jump him again. "Don't you move or I'll shoot you dead."

And he'd a-done it, too. That Charlie was never nearer death than that moment. He thought he was gonna git shot whether he moved or not, fer they was only a few feet apart and Lou couldn't miss.

Charlie backs off, and holds out his hands to show he ain't gonna do nothin'. He never carried a gun like lots of the fellers did, so he was a wide-open target.

Lou gets up, all easy-like a-watchin' Charlie and a-keepin' him in his sights. He sidles over to the bag of gold. When he leans over to pick it up, he clicks off the safety and pulls the trigger. Charlie, bein' young and quick, sees he is gonna shoot, so he drops to the ground and rolls over. He intended to git behind a rock, but doesn't make it. The first bullet misses him, but the second one catches Charlie's sleeve. It only scrapes his arm, bringin' blood, but nothin' serious.

Since Lou is out to kill him, Charlie knows the only way he can save hisself is to go fer Lou. He shore ain't gonna run and leave the gold with Lou. So he figures he can knock him down afore Lou has a chance to fire again. As Lou comes toward him, Charlie digs his heels into the dirt and gives a powerful leap. He rams his head into Lou's stomach. Lou lets out a grunt and buckles over as the gun flies from his hand. But afore the gun left his hand, he pulled the trigger and it fires again, the bullet hittin' Lou's foot.

Lou yells, a-hoppin' on his good foot. The gun is about four feet to his left and the bag of gold to his right. Charlie knows he can't git to the gun afore Lou—it was closer to Lou—so he goes fer the bag of gold. Charlie grabs the bag and a-stumblin', runs down the mountainside. He keeps trippin' and fallin', but still makes headway. Lou meanwhile gets ahold of the gun. Charlie had counted the shots. Only three left. Crippled and swearin' as he was, Lou couldn't catch Charlie. So a-dodgin' back and forth from trees to rocks and missin' two more shots, Charlie soon gits out of gun range. Lou shouts in rage and sends the last bullet after Charlie, who's disappearin' down the mountain with the bag of gold.

When I didn't say anything more, Moss said, "You think that Charlie was Cyrus and Lou was Lem Cowan?"

"Of course. Both names start with the same letters. I never connected it before that Gramps was telling about himself."

"He probably told it in third person so you wouldn't think he stole the gold," Moss said.

"Exactly. When he finished the story, he always asked me, 'Now what do you think Charlie done with the bag of gold?' I'd shake my head, even though he had told me several times before that 'he hightailed it straight to the assayer's office, collected all the money, and left the country.' Gramps always explained further, 'Charlie couldn't give Lou his share of the take or he'd a-got killed. Lou was gonna kill him to take it all, so Charlie jest turned the tables on him.'

" 'Only it wasn't Charlie's fault, was it?' I always had to ask this before Gramps would continue. 'No,' he'd say, 'Charlie had no other choice.' 'And Charlie didn't kill Lou, did he?' I'd ask him.

"Gramps would sigh, sort of in relief, and lean back in the swing. 'No,' he'd say, 'Lou shot his own foot in the struggle. He jest got what was comin' to him.' Then Gramps would give me a self-satisfied smirk that justice had been done and say one of his favorite expressions. 'What crawls under your belly lands on your back.' ''

"So," Moss said, "Charlie, or Cyrus, came back home and built his house and barn with the money?"

I nodded. "That's what I think."

"And Lou, or Lem, after his foot healed, came after him. When Cyrus saw him in his driveway, he knew he was a dead man unless he killed Lem himself. So he somehow got Lem's gun away from him, shot him, and dragged him into the spring cave."

I should have been miserable with this deduction. The concern in Moss's eyes indicated he expected me to be devastated. Instead I was smiling.

"That's what seems the logical explanation, except there's another story Gramps told me that probably explains what came later."

"Was it about the same two men?" Moss didn't understand.

"No. Different names. That's why I never connected them before. But yes, I think it's the same two men. The first story is real, except for the pseudonyms. The geography is probably right. For the second story Gramps changed the names and where it took place so I wouldn't put the stories together. I think that he told me what really happened. And just in case someone ever discovered the body, I would know the true story."

I was feeling better all the time as I sorted out in my mind the details of the second story.

"Well, are you going to tell me?" Moss asked.

Chapter Twelve

"Gramps would tell me his stories at various places," I said to Moss. The sun was low, a red ball disappearing behind a bank of clouds straight down the road ahead of us. "In good weather it was often in the porch swing. He probably told this second one to me there, also, the other one with a partner in it, but I remember one particular time when he told it we were milking in the barn. I don't know how it happened, because usually there were other people around, but this time it was just the two of us. Aunt Iris usually did the milking, but this time she must have been away from home helping out a sick neighbor. She did that lots. Anyway, Gramps was milking Sycamore and I was trying ineffectively to squeeze some milk out of Redbud. . . ."

"Those were names of cows?"

"Yes." I laughed. "He named his daughters after

flowers and his cows after trees. There was Dogwood, Persimmon, and Hickory that I remember.''

''And he still milked by hand?''

''Yes. He didn't take well to modern equipment. They didn't sell milk anymore. Just milked for their own use.''

Moss shook his head at this evidence of old-fashioned farming and living. ''Go on with your story.''

''It was late fall and cold outside, but comfortable in the lower level of the barn because of the heat from the horses in their stalls and the other cattle loafing in the shed.

''Gramps's cheek pressed against Sycamore's side, and he faced me while squatting on the low milking stool. Strong spurts of milk sang against the metal bucket keeping time to Gramps's story, slow when he was describing something and splashing full force during the fight scenes. When he finished the story, the pail was three-fourths full of white, foamy milk.''

In my mind I heard the wind whistling around the barn accompanied by an undertone of contented cows munching their grain and an occasional stomp or snort from one of the horses. Almost like Gramps bending over his bucket that evening twenty years ago, I leaned over in the seat of Moss's convertible. ''This is the story he told me.''

The fall of the year like it is now, Red Rose, puts me in mind of what happened to a feller I knowed about back in Colorado. That was many years ago. Long ago. Actually the story is about two fellers that used to be partners. Now the first feller, name of Clark, mined him some gold, enough to buy hisself a spread up in the mountains in a fine little valley with a creek and a good bottom field. First he built a big barn and then fer his family he built a fine house. I tell you, now he was set up fine. He had him a good woman and three little youngsters and another on the way. Everythin' was goin' great guns fer him. He had the world by the tail with a downhill pull.

Then one day while he was a-buildin' a fence around the yard to keep the chickens out of the flowers, he seen this here feller ride up on a bay horse. He recognized him right off as a partner he had for a time. Mainly it was on a trappin' trip, but they done some prospectin' together, too. But they parted on not too good terms. Then later when Clark found him a gold claim that produced, the other feller tried to git in on that, too, a-causin' him some trouble and tryin' to take over the claim.

Now back home when Clark sees this ornery piece of humanity come up to his place, comin' all this way to find him, he knows he is up to no good. So Clark drops his shovel and crowbar he was using to dig out a posthole, and thrusts his hammer in the loop of his overalls so that in case they's trouble he'll have somethin' to protect hisself with. He runs down the road to meet him afore he gits to the house, fer he ain't about to let him git anywheres near his family.

"You ain't welcome here, Luke," Clark yells at him when he gits near enough fer him to hear him.

"I come after the gold you stole from my claim," Luke shouts back at Clark, reinin' his horse and jumpin' off. He is half drunk and sways a bit. He is mad-der'n . . . he is mad enough to chew splinters.

"That wasn't yer claim," Clark yells back. "I filed legal on it."

I won't tell you, Red Rose, what that filthy-mouthed Luke said. Ain't proper fer a little girl's ears. He swears and bellows so much that Clark eases his hammer out of its loop in his overalls leg jest in case. The feller was lower'n a hog's belly and Clark knowed it.

"Git off my land," Clark orders, holdin' up the hammer to show he means business. Clark figures Luke is carryin' a gun, so he is a-watchin' ready to jump if necessary. Luke wore one of them long, cover-up slickers men in the West wear, so Clark couldn't see if he had a gun.

"Not till you give me my gold," Luke yells. Then he makes a quick movement with his right hand to push aside his coat. He isn't as quick as Clark, 'cause as soon as the pistol clears the holster from under the coat, Clark throws his hammer at Luke's gun hand. It hits his mark, business end of the hammer square across his knuckles. Luke yells out as the pistol goes a-spinnin' outta his hand and lands a few feet away. The gun fires when it hits the ground, but the bullet don't hit nothin'. Buries itself in the dirt.

Things really git lively. Both men dive fer the pis-tol. Bein' closer, Luke gits there first. He sprawls over the gun and grabs it in his left hand, 'cause his right hind was hurt bad. A split second later, Clark is on top of him. They wrestle there in the drive, a-kickin' and a-poundin' each other. They roll over, down into a little holler. While they's fightin', Luke is tryin' to point the pistol at Clark while Clark is tryin' to wrest it away. But he can't get ahold of it. Luke moves his hand around too fast for Clark to hold on to it. Once he manages to grab the barrel, but Luke has an iron grip on it. All Clark can do is push the barrel away from him back against Luke's body.

The gun fires again. Luke jerks, his face goes blank, and he slumps in Clark's arms. Dead. Clark pulls back Luke's coat and sees blood a-comin' outta his chest. In the fight over the gun, Luke shoots himself right in the heart. He is gone jest like that. Even with Luke dead, Clark has to pry the pistol out of Luke's hand.

Now Clark was in a dilemma. He wasn't concerned about the feller gittin' killed, fer he was a worthless skunk. Clark got out without gittin' shot and he got hold of the gun, but here was this dead feller right by his front yard. Of course, the feller was trespassin', and he was the one that pulled the gun and then shot hisself, but would anybody believe that? Nobody seen him come. Nobody seen him try to kill Clark but shoot hisself instead. As far as Clark knowed, the feller had no family or friends, so nobody would come lookin' fer him.

If the law come, he'd have a heap of explainin' to do. The sheriff'd go snoopin' around lookin' fer more proof than jest Clark's word of what happened. He didn't want none of that fuss. It would upset his family. But what really worried him was that he wasn't fer certain sure that his claim was legally his. Him and Luke had filed jointly on several claims. An inquiry might find that Luke had also filed on this last one and that some of the gold did belong to him. He was sure that wasn't the case, but there was that naggin' doubt. Gittin' the law in would open up a heap of trouble he didn't want. The money was long since gone, spent on his land and house.

Clark knows he can't chance no investigation. So he looks toward his house. Nobody in sight. He looks over at the barn. Nobody there. He lets out a sigh of relief. His wife and young'uns hadn't seen the feller come. Them hearin' the gunshots didn't worry him none, 'cause they wouldn't think nothin' 'bout them. Common. Lots of hunters in the area.

The two men had rolled outta sight down the brushy slope into a hollowed-out place. Now Clark, he runs back to where he was buildin' his fence to git his shovel and crowbar, a-fixin on diggin' a grave quick-like, or at least covering up the body until he could do somethin' more permanent with it. But first he catches Luke's bay horse and puts him in his barn along with several others he was tradin'. Can't let a riderless horse run loose. Folks would wonder.

Then back at the holler, he drags the body a few feet to a spot under a rocky ledge overhang that was sort of like a cave. He digs the hole out some more. He takes off Luke's spurs, thrusts the still-warm gun in his back pocket, and drags the body inside. It's as good a place as a six-foot-under grave. Then he blocks up the openin'. He figures that no one will ever know.

I paused. Moss seemed to know that I wasn't finished, so he said nothing, but his eyes sparkled with excitement and he was grinning. So was I. We both knew that Gramps was exonerated in the murder.

Everything we already knew fit with the two stories that involved a partner. Moss glanced quickly at me before he slowly passed a farmer on a tractor. After cresting a hill and seeing a clear highway ahead, he resumed speed.

I continued, "Gramps always stopped right there in the story to let me ask, 'Did anyone ever find Luke's body?'

" 'No.' Gramps shook his head and then added, 'Not that I ever heard tell, anyways. Not yit.' "

Moss said when he was sure I was finished, "His story gives all the important details, right down to the broken right hand, the spurs, the pistol, and the bay horse."

"The differences were probably so that I wouldn't put them together and connect them with Gramps. The names and the locations were different so that I wouldn't think these were the same men."

"And instead of the partner trying to get away with all the gold as in the first story," Moss said, "in the second he tried to jump the claim. But the result was the same. Lem Cowan, alias Lou/Luke, was the villain. He initiated the fight and lost both times."

"And though I didn't know it, Gramps told me exactly how it happened. I knew all along!"

"Iris indicated that you were special to him, and you were probably the one most interested in the place. That's why he kept telling you his stories."

"Probably."

"But why didn't he keep it to himself? Why tell anyone?"

I had to think about that for a minute. "He was very

knowledgeable about the geology of this land. He knew that springs sometimes dry up, or go underground, like his spring did. Given the right conditions they might surface again. If the environment around his spring changed, the bones would be exposed.''

"Or if someone used earth-moving equipment around the spring like I did,'' Moss said.

"He knew that something like that could happen. And if it did, the physical evidence would point to him as the murderer.''

"So he disguised the stories enough that you wouldn't connect them to him, yet you would figure them out later if the body was exposed and he was accused.'' He looked at me in wonder. "What a clever man! That is just what has happened now. As an outsider, I certainly suspected him, and so did both you and Iris.''

"But why tell me? Why not Aunt Iris or one of his sons?''

"You were better insurance. Being so young, you would live longer. You said you listened to him more than the others, didn't you?''

"Yes, my cousins enjoyed his stories the first time, but not over and over. They just melted away when he'd get going. Aunt Iris was always too busy. She brushed him off when he started.''

"So you were the obvious one to tell.''

"We've got to tell Aunt Iris.''

Moss agreed.

It had been a perfect day. Though tired, neither of us wanted it to end. Since on the way home we drove through The Grove, just a couple of blocks from Aunt Iris's house, we stopped to tell her.

When we were ready to leave her house, Iris looked ten years younger. We knew that she would no longer have her nightmares, and the fond memories of her father would remain.

The three of us were almost giddy. Lem Cowan's ghost had no further power. The evil he forced on Gramps colored his whole life. Wanting a better life for his family, he used money that did not belong to him and concealed a death. No wonder he often warned us about the danger of the cave. The danger was not only a physical one, but one that if discovered would ruin the Loveland family. Presenting himself to everyone as a strong and in-charge man, he knew every day what was buried inside himself and the spring cave. Making his portion of the world more beautiful with plants was one of his ways of atoning. Another way was telling his stories over and over. And I alone of his large family listened.

Rest easy, Gramps, we understand, I spoke inwardly. *Only Aunt Iris, Moss, and I know, and we will keep your secret forever. We know now that you are no murderer, only human.*

Although Aunt Iris was completely innocent of anything, the evil affected her. Suffering alone for eighty years with the fear of her father's sin was a horror she had never been able to shake. Now the shadow was gone.

Moss and I? The loss of the buildings had kept me distant even as we were getting closer. Finding the skeleton was the first occurrence that drew us together.

Then just as with Aunt Iris, the fear of what Gramps might have done held me aloof. Now both Aunt Iris and I felt like floating, our relief was so great.

As we rose to leave Aunt Iris's house, she took Moss's arm, turned him around to look straight into his eyes, and said with tears in her eyes, "I can't tell you how grateful I am to you. Though at first I could have drowned you in your horrid pond, now I bless you for building it. Because of what you uncovered on the farm, you have put to rest my lifelong doubts. It is right that the buildings should be gone, since they were built with partly stolen money. Though I can see that my father really didn't have any other choice. I'm grateful to you for bringing all that to light."

"I didn't . . ."

Aunt Iris didn't let him finish. "Darrah tells me that the spring is once again flowing, even creating an ever-running stream. She says the lake area is becoming beautiful with all of her designs and plantings. Papa loved plants. They were his therapy. Therefore, Darrah's plantings and landscaping are a much more fitting memorial to him and to the Loveland family than some old buildings that were built with partly stolen money. And when Darrah's work is all finished, I want to go back one more time to see it."

She did a rare thing for her. She kissed him on his cheek. I don't remember her kissing me since I was a little girl.

"Thank you," she said.

Then she turned to me and said right in front of Moss as if he weren't there, "Darrah girl, I told you from the first that this was a desirable man, didn't I?"

I glanced at Moss's amused face. "I think, Aunt Iris, that your words were to the effect that he's got money because of his designer clothes. You also said that he's a fine-looking fellow and that he wasn't wearing a wedding ring."

"Exactly. And doesn't that makes him desirable at first glance? Proof that you thought so, too, is that you remembered exactly what I said. That counts for something." She turned to Moss in an aside. "She liked what she saw, too."

I stammered, "I did not. I . . ."

Moss was grinning, his little-boy enjoyment of our conversation evident.

"Now, Darrah girl," Aunt Iris said, interrupting me, "I see that he's even better than I first thought. He's kind and considerate. He is sensitive and smart. You make a fine team. I think the two of you together could do anything you wanted to do."

"Aunt Iris, please . . ."

Aunt Iris turned to Moss with an impish look in her eyes. "Darrah is embarrassed. You aren't, are you?"

"Not a bit. I'm enjoying this immensely."

"My father would like you. And you would have liked him." Then to me she said, "He's perfect. Don't let him get away."

"Aunt Iris!"

"I won't go away," Moss said. The corners of his mouth curved up irresistibly.

"She's the best of the Lovelands," Aunt Iris said. Now she was talking to him as if I weren't there. "My father knew it and was partial to her." She continued, including both of us but looking at Moss. "I grew up and lived in a different world than you two. I really had no choice but to stay home and help out. There was a young man very much like you, Moss, that came around some. But I didn't encourage him. I couldn't leave my parents with all those children and work to do. They needed me. I thought in a few years I could leave them. But the time never came. They always needed me. The young man quit coming and married a girl across the river.''

''I never knew that!'' I said.

Aunt Iris gave me a glance that indicated that I never asked. She was right. All of us took her for granted, a fixture at the Loveland farm. We never wondered what she might have wanted for herself.

She continued speaking to Moss. Her eyes were intent, forcing him to understand where she was going with this conversation. ''I don't regret doing that. I've guided my brothers and sisters and their children and grandchildren. My parents' lives were financially safer and more comfortable because I was always with them, helping with the farming, the accounts, the housework, and chores.

''But I missed out on much. These past few days, since you and Darrah found that body, I've wondered if my life was wasted, helping my father when it appeared that he had built his life on murder. Now tonight''—she squeezed my hand, though she still didn't look at me—''because of Darrah's remembering those stories that he never told me, or anyone else that I know of, I know that my single life wasn't for nothing. But I don't want Darrah to live as I did. It worries me that she is so focused on her business and proving to herself and everyone else that she can do it, that she is missing out on the same things that I did.

"Only she has a choice that I didn't have. Today she can have a career *and* a partner to share her life with. Things have changed so much since I was Darrah's age." Aunt Iris paused, chuckled, and continued speaking to Moss. "Did you know that my mother was thirty years old before women could vote? I remember that first election. It was about the time Papa finished our house. Even then most of the women in the neighborhood didn't go vote. Mama did and Papa was proud of her."

Ignoring me, she seemed to change the subject. "Her name, Darrah, is Irish. Did you know that?"

"No, but I'm not surprised," Moss said. "It sounds Irish. And with her beautiful red hair and fair complexion, I figured there was some Irish in her background."

"In Irish spelling it has a G in it—D-a-r-r-a-G-h. The name means wealthy. I helped name her."

"I didn't know that," I said. I felt like crying out, *Remember me? I'm here!*

Aunt Iris just nodded her head at me but continued speaking to Moss. "When she was born with all that bright red hair, we all looked for a beautiful name that would express the great richness she brought us. Papa wanted to call her Rose. But we thought there were enough flowers in the family. Since her mother was Irish, she and I picked Darrah."

"Why hadn't anyone told me before?" I asked.

Aunt Iris said to me as if I were a pesky child that had to be quieted, "I guess there wasn't any reason that you needed to know it. But now Moss needs to know the wealth that is here for him.'' She turned back to him.

''I already knew,'' Moss said quietly. ''If I didn't know it that day on the hillside when I almost ran into you, I knew it in the country store when I formally met her and learned who she was. I was struck right away.''

''Then prove it,'' Aunt Iris ordered in the same tone of voice she used with us children when telling us to be polite and say please or thank you. ''While I'm still kicking and have my right mind, kiss her and ask her to marry you.''

That is exactly what he did right there in Aunt Iris's doorway.

Chapter Thirteen

The next April once again I took my great-aunt back to the old Loveland farm. Just as in the fall when we last drove the route together, Aunt Iris's head moved from side to side, her eyes missing nothing. As before, she was excited and looking forward to cresting the hill for the view of the valley. This time she was fore-warned and prepared.

While we were still on the blacktop, she waved at our cousin as we passed his place with all the silos. He was opening a gate to let his Holstein herd out onto the new spring pasture. He waved back eagerly and indicated that he'd soon follow us. The Carlton house, the one that saddened her in the first trip be-cause it was so deteriorated, had given up the struggle over the winter and fallen down. Only one leaning wall covered with Virginia creeper still remained standing. A low cluster of blooming dogwood and the small, newly formed leaves of the oaks leaning over the ruins tried to camouflage the neglect.

Farther down the highway, Elbow Jurgen's neat buildings made Iris smile because on the north side of his house were the beginnings of a room addition for his grandson's new baby. There was no sign of anyone there, for the family was probably inside getting ready. A few weeks before, I had learned the special position that Elbow held in the community until he retired a few years back. Moss was the one who told me. The two men, separated by sixty years and very different backgrounds, found many interests in common and quickly became good friends.

When I told Aunt Iris about Elbow, she looked at me as if I had just discovered that the sun rose every morning. "Of course, child. *Everyone* knows that." Since I remembered so much from my childhood, she assumed that I knew all about the people in the neighborhood. What I remembered were my great-grandparents and my experiences with the extended Loveland family on their farm. When I was eight years old, the neighbors and their activities were unimportant to me.

When we passed Elbow's place, I asked Aunt Iris, "Are you sure Elbow's coming?" I was nervous that everything would go well.

"Don't worry so much. He'll be there. He wouldn't miss it for anything. He was very pleased that Moss asked him."

"Of course. He's part of it."

Leaving the blacktop and crossing the cattle guard onto the lane along the ridge, we entered a different world from the one we saw on the trip we made in the fall. At that time leaves were falling, grasses were browning, and squirrels were gathering nuts for the winter. Though the weather was still mild then, the threat of winter's chill was in the air. Today all nature was exploding with newness, growth, and vigor. We spotted some wild turkeys and heard the flutelike whistle of orioles. We saw a variety of wildflowers along the sides of the lane—spring beauty, spiderwort, shooting stars, and wake-robin. The blossoms of the redbud were fading, but the greening woods were full of dogwood. The trees appeared covered with snow, the layers of blossoms were so prolific. And though the breeze entering my opened windows was mild, it still held a hint of the winter's chill that was rapidly leaving the land.

When we turned off onto the driveway down to the farm, as I did last fall, I paused again to view our favorite scene. Though Aunt Iris wouldn't miss this day for anything, and had thoroughly enjoyed the ride so far, she became a bit anxious when we turned the corner and I braked to a stop. We looked across the steep meadow blanketed with new grass and spotted with lavender patches of sweet William that moved with the breeze. Aunt Iris's fingers were entwined as she held them in front of her, ready to cover her face as she did before. Instead, she let out a gasp of pleasure and grabbed the skirt of my new dress. Then she straightened in the seat and patted my leg reassuringly.

"It's wonderful, Darrah," she said. I looked at her beaming face and her white hair that she had curled slightly so that it curved under, framing her face, not every which way as it usually was. The last time I remembered her fixing her hair was at Gramps's funeral. She was attractive in her new blue dress and navy spring coat.

We both looked down to the scene below us. Dominating the view was the rich new green surrounding the sparkling lake and the brooklet that flowed from it down the slope into the recently cultivated field. Winding around the lake was the drive that crossed a wooden bridge and led to the bluff hill beyond. The freshness so evident in the meadow before us spread over the entire area, interrupted in places with natural-looking rocky outcroppings, clumps of white and pink flowering bushes, and groves of young trees.

"It's magic," she said, imitating my businesslike telephone greeting. We both laughed.

"Yes, it really is, isn't it," I said eagerly, "how everything has worked out?" I wasn't referring only to the landscaping.

Under the largest walnut tree, where Moss, Connie, and I ate our first lunch together, were some folding chairs. I had hoped to arrive first to show Aunt Iris everything before the others arrived, but Connie and Moss beat us. I spotted our business pickup parked beside Moss's convertible. Connie, with her current boyfriend, was already setting up a portable table for the refreshments. Neither Moss nor I wanted anything, but she had insisted. "It's part of my responsibility," she had told us. With Connie it is better to go along with her than to try to convince her otherwise. Trust her to always see that there was food for any occasion.

Even though I had been at the farm many times

during the six months, overseeing and doing much of the work, I saw the great change as if for the first time through Aunt Iris's eyes. She liked it! Just like her, I was almost awed by the transformation. Waves of pleasure swept over me. We hugged each other before I drove on down the hill.

Moss must have seen us pause up on the ridge, because by the time we drove down the hill to the entrance, he was there to greet us. I didn't know which sight was the most beautiful, the lake area in all its spring glory or Moss. His hair, without his customary cap, was shaped to enhance its natural wave. Full on the top and sides, it framed the strong features of his face. His new, tailored brown suit matched his hair and eyes. In spite of how well it fit his body to invite the eye to linger on his slim, erect form, the light blues and greens in his tie directed the beholder's eye to his shining face.

He hurried to my open window, leaned in to kiss me, and reaching over me, clasped Aunt Iris's hand. The shining look on her face told him that she approved. He gave me a look that showed his relief and said to her, "I'm so glad you feel well enough to come. It means everything to us that you are here."

"I'd come even if I had to get up from my deathbed," she said, her voice strong and cocky. "Now, young man, show me what Darrah's magic touch has done to the place before everyone else gets here."

I scooted over on the seat for Moss to drive. Slowly and with great care to avoid every plant and carefully positioned rock, he drove over the lake area. We wanted Aunt Iris to see everything—the mass of pink azaleas from the shut-ins, whose blossoms covered the bank of the brook near the bridge; the grove of wild black cherries; the wild plum thicket in full bloom; the hornbeam trees; and the four river birch we transplanted from the slough. Mayapples, birdfoot violets, columbine, and Dutchman's-breeches bloomed in natural-appearing spots throughout. New fronds of ferns curled up out of the ground. Young patches of reeds thrived along the brook. In a few quiet pools we pointed out to her the beginnings of watercress and duckweed. Young oaks, hickory, maples, sycamores, and shortleaf pine were already at home in various locations throughout the area. The once-ugly bareness was rich with color and life.

I anxiously watched Aunt Iris for any signs of sadness or regret. I didn't see any. Instead, her wrinkled face was as eager as a girl's. With one hand on the assist handle above her and the other clutching my leg, she looked at everything, her mouth held in a perpetual, unvoiced "Oh." She delighted in calling out the names of many of the plants, while I identified others. I showed her where we planted flowers and forbs that would mature in other seasons.

"No daffodils or hollyhocks that would remind me of home?" Iris asked.

"No," I said, "but that wasn't the reason we didn't plant them."

"I wanted only native plants," Moss explained.

"Everything is so new now that it looks like a cultivated garden, but as the plants grow, they will give the untouched, natural appearance that our first ancestors saw when they came to this country."

"Except for the lake?" Aunt Iris asked.

Moss laughed. "Yes, the lake is not natural, though it will look that way in a few years when the vegetation grows. But the stream is natural. Your ancestors saw a spring branch here about where it is now until it petered out and was covered up. We just opened it."

"And it came back to life," I said.

"It's all right, Moss." She leaned over me to tap his shoulder. "I know you and Darrah have been worried about how I'll take all these changes. Don't let my feelings bother you one minute longer. With all of this richness and vitality in their place, I'm okay with the fact that the buildings are gone. Really, I am, now that I know my father's complete story. It's right that all the evidence is wiped away. The buildings were remnants of my father's greed—or perhaps a better word would be his dishonesty—of keeping more than his half from the gold mines. Now that the house and barn are gone, it sort of cancels that out."

"And the lake?" I asked. "Are you all right with the lake?"

"Yes, even the lake is good." She wiped her face with the handkerchief she clutched in her hand. "It washes away Papa's mistake of hiding the body. That's what I call what he did, a mistake. Not a crime. In building the lake, Moss, you cleared away the bad part of Papa's life and allowed the spring to come out of hiding. Just like the truth that Papa concealed has come out. Think how hard it must have been for him to keep those secrets all those years."

She paused. Tightening her grip on my leg, she continued, "The way I see it is that an evil man choked up the spring, not the rubbish in the ditch. Getting rid of the litter let the spring flow and also let the truth come out. The spring has washed away my fears."

She lifted her hands to help us understand what she was saying. "I sound like a poet, but do you know what I mean?" We both nodded. "My father is gone, and I'm old and will soon join him and my mother. I'm sure Mama must have known his secret because they shared everything. Perhaps that was the strain of sadness that ran through their lives, even when things were going well for them. They and I, all three of us, in our own ways learned to live with our secrets."

"They had each other. But Aunt Iris, you were all alone with your secret fear. You've thought all these years that your father was a murderer."

"No. I hid it away. I convinced myself it was only a nightmare. But that's over now with a satisfactory-enough ending."

We rode in silence for a few seconds while we admired the shiny new, moss-green leaves of the black haw. Aunt Iris said, "Moss, the best result of all from your building the lake and opening up the spring was that it brought you two together."

Moss gave his beautiful, full-blown smile and squeezed my hand. Aunt Iris didn't miss our shared look. "I'm right about that. If you two had not found Lem Cowan's body, I don't think that Darrah would ever have forgiven you for the buildings."

"Iris," he said, "you are a remarkably perceptive woman."

She grinned, pleased with his compliment. "Let's

cut out all of this nonsense. Darrah's dilemma has been resolved. So now, are you two going to show me the rest of the farm?''

After making a quick run to the river and then up onto the bluff pasture, Moss drove to the walnut tree area and parked my car beside his. He helped Aunt Iris into one of the folding chairs. Her back was to the forested ridge where the drive turns off the ridge to the farm. Without moving her position in the chair, she could view the lake and entrance area which was below and slightly to her right. Straight ahead was the panorama of the bottom fields and the trees bordering the river. Turning her head to the left she could see the steep, almost nonexistent bluff trail climbing to the ridge pasture.

She sighed in contentment. ''I can see Papa everywhere. I feel closer to him than I have since his death.'' She shook her head slowly, looking from side to side in amazement. ''He told me many times that his Red Rose was the pick of the litter. He would be so proud of you, Darrah.''

I was pleased that she thought Gramps would like what we did. She knew him better than anyone still living. In spite of everything we recently learned about him and even after all the years since his death, I still needed his approval.

''You really think so? He wouldn't mind about the house and barn?''

''No, I don't think so. He told you his stories so you would know what he did. He knew that one day you would figure it out and somehow make it right. You were his hope for clearing his conscience. I think that he would be okay with the house being gone, and he'd be especially happy that the spring is once again alive. But even more important than all that, like me, Darrah, he would be glad that you and Moss found each other.''

This was the third time she had said my name without tagging on ''girl.'' Ever since I could remember, whenever she spoke directly to me, she ran together ''Darrahgirl'' as if it was one word. Apparently in her mind, I was finally fully grown up. The way she said my name now was like she was passing to me the family leadership.

Elbow and his grandson and family were the first of the guests to arrive. I hardly recognized him in his dark suit and tie. He even wore his false teeth which gave his always-pleasant face a fuller appearance. After we admired the new baby and his mother sat down with him in one of the scattered chairs, Elbow, still standing, visited with Aunt Iris.

''These young people doing all this planting around the place makes me remember little things about your dad I hadn't thought of for years,'' he said.

''Me, too,'' Aunt Iris said. ''Can you believe that this is the first time I've actually set foot on the farm since I left all those years ago?''

Elbow nodded. ''Yeah, I know. Lots of changes.'' He glanced around smiling. ''Mostly for the best, I'd say.'' Aunt Iris nodded agreement. ''Young Wright here says that I can use his boat to fish in the lake when the bass and perch he stocked in there grow some. Getting down to the river is becoming harder and harder for me these days.'' He chuckled and laid his hand on Aunt Iris's walker. "You know what I mean?"

"I certainly do."

"Your dad, ol' Cyrus, was a good, God-fearing man. Always a great friend to me even when I was a little shaver."

"Yes, I remember. He thought a lot of you. Almost like you were one of his sons."

"We'd talk when I tagged around after him. He kept me out of trouble. He'd listen to my dreams. Encouraged me to get an education and make something of myself." He paused to watch a few cars arrive. "I said at his funeral how he was always ready to give a hand to his neighbors. Yeah, a good man. You know, once he even gave me a fancy bridle and told me to sell it and pay for some classes I was wanting to take."

"I never knew that," Aunt Iris said.

Moss and I were all attentive when he mentioned a valuable bridle.

"Did he say where he got it?" I asked.

"Yeah. From his Western days. He said he got it off of a guy who mistreated his horse. Too fancy, Cyrus said, for 'round here. I did like he told me and sold it. I got a hundred dollars and paid for that first summer's expenses, tuition, board, and all. I told him he ought to give it to Arnie, but he said I was the logical one to have it. I never did understand why."

I knew why. Elbow had seen the stranger from the West. Also, helping with Elbow's education would help ease Gramps's guilt.

"What did the bridle look like?" Moss asked.

"The finest leather, and tooled all over, except the reins. The metal on it was silver." Elbow smiled at Aunt Iris, his lined face handsome under his mass of white hair. "It had one of those spade bits." He turned to Moss to explain. "The kind that has a high port that gouges the horse's tongue when you pull on the reins. Often makes them bleed at the mouth. Cyrus gave me another bit to replace the spade bit. He didn't want anyone to use the brutal one."

Though we didn't say anything out loud, Moss, Aunt Iris, and I all knew that we each were thinking the same thing: the bridle came from the bay horse that Lem Cowan was riding. This was still further proof of the body's identity and Cyrus's involvement.

Elbow grinned and said to me, "Did you know that ol' Cyrus was the one that gave me my nickname, Elbow?"

"No. I always wondered how you got that name."

"I was forever hanging 'round him, asking him all kinds of questions, especially about his days in the West. He started calling me Elbow because I was always elbowing in on everyone's conversations, asking questions." He laughed. "He was right. But asking questions and being a good listener has helped me out all these years. I guess the name fit, because that's what everyone calls me. Not many even know my real name."

Allen, Carl, and the other workers soon arrived. Allen stationed himself by the entrance to show people where to park. Not everyone was as careful where they walked and drove as we were. Under the walnut tree, Abby and more of my relatives and some of Moss's friends soon gathered around the few chairs. Acting the part of hostess while putting final touches to the table of refreshments, Connie directed people toward the chairs, seating the oldest or those with young children. Underfoot the soft bluegrass had grown to just the perfect height of a mowed lawn, its softness unmarred by cutting. Buttercups, violets, and the pinkish-white blossoms of rue anemone peeked out from the grass. Around the trunk of one of the trees was a clump of red columbine and the shiny, umbrellalike leaves of half a dozen mayapple plants.

The breeze brought the sweet scent from the wild plums as everyone gathered. Moss and I introduced people. Almost everyone hugged me, and all the women hugged Moss.

"Ready?" Moss whispered to me when there was a pause in my conversation with cousin Abby who was giving me a detailed account of another cousin's latest operation.

I nodded. Finished with arranging the special centerpiece and placing chips, mints, and nuts around it, Connie checked me out. She pushed back the errant strand of hair that always fell over my eye, brushed off my white dress, and straightened my pearls. The breeze immediately blew the hair back over my forehead. "I guess you'll do." She laughed, flipping her long hair over her shoulder. "At least you aren't wearing that floppy hat." I admitted that I looked halfway refined in a rather feminine-looking dress instead of my standard navy-striped shirt and black jeans.

Moss stood in front of me. Like Connie did, he pushed the strand of hair off my forehead and looked into my eyes. He said just the one word, "Darrah," rolling the Rs in his special way. He took my hand.

I remembered the beauty we had both admired that was created by the rushing water of Rocky Oak Shut-Ins as it pushed through the hard granite obstruction rather than detouring around it. Moss was right that day when he said that I was stubborn like the water. And like it, by persisting, pushing through the hard truth, I found beauty beyond my imagination.

The chatting of the guests hushed. They moved aside to make an aisle. To the music of the rustle of new leaves, the toads calling from the lake, the buzz of honeybees busy burying themselves in the buttercups, and a distant call of the turtledove, we walked together on the bluegrass carpet toward Elbow Jurgen. With patches of sunlight dancing over his head, he stood tall and dignified, as befitted his role of justice of the peace, holding an open book in his hands.

He smiled at each of us and paused dramatically before he said, "Do you, Darrah Loveland, take this man, Moss Wright . . ."